MW01632522

THE WILD CALL OF NATURE

Adrián Villasenor-Galarza

LIVING FLAMES
BOOKS

LIVING FLAMES
BOOKS

Illustrations: Luis Fika

ISBN: 978-1-7358322-1-0

For Iyari Ananda, the little, white hummingbird.
May you fly free and wild amidst the jungles
of the Great Mystery.

Table of Contents

1. SACRED OBLIVION 3

2. ROUTINE AND CEMENT 9

3. CHRONICLES OF THE BLOOMING EARTH 15

4. COUNCIL OF ALL BEINGS 23

5. REUNION 31

6. THE SPELL OF THE MACHINE WORLD 39

7. BIRD'S-EYE VIEW 47

8. ANCESTRAL MUTANT JUNGLE 55

9. THE MISTERY OF THE WORLDS 63

10. MEDICINE FOR THE BROKEN 71

11. COSMIC TRIBE 79

12. INFINITE WILD GLOW 87

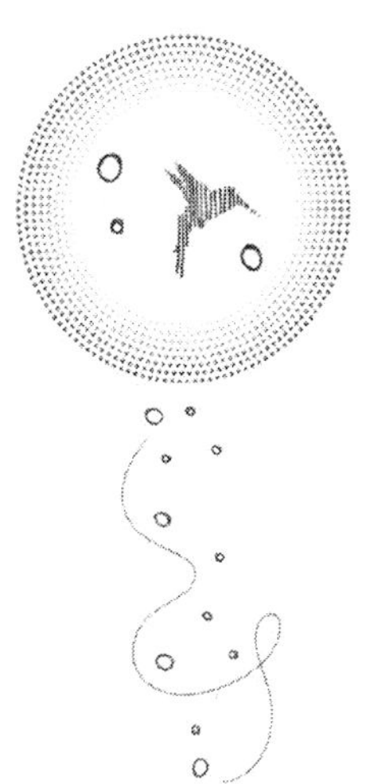

1

1.
SACRED OBLIVION

The expanding universe is the abode of this sacred being in which transformation and regeneration occur in an endless net of cycles. It is a whole world of change and innovation where life, as we know it, exists.

Navigating the immensity of the cosmos, water, air, fire, and earth—accompanied by a mysterious force that animates them from within—come together to create some of the most astounding forms, patterns, and landscapes ever witnessed.

Both miracles and calamities are born out of this planetary creature, brimming with the light of life and its faithful companion, death, embarked on their eternal, breathtaking dance. The essence of this great being is enveloped in legends of fire, rock, and lightning, making its way through enigmas such as the origin of life and the occurrence of consciousness.

Here, on planet Earth, there is paramount beauty, often enveloped in uncertainty and wonder. Unpredictable events and seemingly meaningless situations tirelessly emerge from the web of relations amongst the countless creatures that populate the many Earthly realms.

An infinite number of events occur in unison at any given point in time. Tiny winged beings laugh and fly around leafy trees, while elusive earthworms slide through the passages and tunnels of the dark, food-rich topsoil. Like out of nowhere, strong, pulsating vibrations are felt by the soil's countless inhabitants, coming from the tapping of small human feet joyfully running toward the river.

Immersed in their play and determination to take off their clothes to take a dip in the cool waters, the children pass by a commanding limestone rock formation. The ancestral rock, patient geological witness, exhibits a variety of old traces of life throughout its body: mollusks, corals, mosses, algae, and more. Life and time transformed into stone.

Meanwhile, a horned owl perched on the upper branches of a robust and vigorous oak tree is awakened by the children's playful voices. As she opens her penetrating eyes for a few moments, she notices the distinctive organizational skills of a row of ants, to then return to her peaceful sleep.

At the oak's base, just above an extensive network of filaments that attest to the widespread fungi intelligence, lies a small red door with a shiny golden knob that seems to go straight to the core of the vibrant tree. In reality, the door serves as the entrance to the cozy home of chubby little creatures with red hats, big rounded noses, and a great sense of humor.

These astute, elusive beings are known as the forest keepers due to their daily patrolling and protection of their homelands. They are diligent workers who watch over the safety and wellbeing of each and every member of the forest, constantly expressing their gratitude and fortune for undertaking such an honorable task.

The sun shines serenely in the celestial vault. Black and blue butterflies flutter around taking their daily light bath, while pollinating and taking their food from vivacious orange flowers.

A noisy flock of ringed-tailed coatis goes up and down stones and branches, smelling here and there in search of fruits, seeds, and other foods of their liking. Small, fast-moving birds traverse the sky in a "V" shape, displaying prodigious dexterity and coordination, just as if they were one multi-being.

In all its interdependent splendor, the forest dances to the rhythm and flow of the Sun's energy, activating a variety of processes that feed and uplift the majesty and revered expression of the forest's natural symphony.

In a few moments, the exquisite co-existence of the forest gives way to a pervading sense of change and uncertainty. Threatening grey clouds accompanied by lightning coalesce vertiginously in the West, announcing the arrival of a great storm.

The children are gone, and the whole ecosystem patiently awaits the water festival. It is well known by all community members that rain brings about life, so they rejoice in its presence.

Meanwhile, the forest keepers become aware that something much more dangerous than the storm is fast-approaching. This sensation is particularly felt in their small, puffy chests. Given the urgency and magnitude of such sensation, the forest keepers rush to give notice to the great web of forest life—a message that reverberates in the circles of keepers of Earth's diverse ecosystems.

A group of self-adoring human mammals arrive at the forest equipped with noisy metal weapons of all kinds, huge trucks, and lots of smoke. The pack of humans yell incessantly to each other under the great curtain of water that bathes the region. They are about to "clean up" the area and, no obstacle, including rain, stops them in fulfilling their task.

A renowned development company acquired the forest to build an array of grey, square, and lifeless structures for people to live in. Humans, motivated by small plastic-like rectangles on which they base their existence referred to as "money," crush, lacerate, mutilate, and murder the creatures of the forest until only a handful of oak trees remain standing. Some forest creatures manage to flee, although the vast majority fall victim to the ecocide.

As this all happens, the keepers of the forest evoke their power to make themselves visible to the looters' eyes. A dialogue ought to take place. Sadly, the chubby beings' efforts are in vain. Humans are simply not able to see them—they're so numb they barely listen to themselves.

The forest keepers experience first-hand what they've been hearing for a long time. A considerable portion of the human family has lost the ability to communicate with the prodigious diversity of non-human beings and nature's subtle presences. Human faculties are sorely atrophied.

In the eyes of the money-worshipping mammal, the universe revolves around violence, domination, and control, all taking place on an exclusively material plane. Nature plainly exists to serve them.

The so-called civilized human is largely unable to find meaning and value in the bird's song, in the powerful magnetic influence of the moon, or in the wild flow of the peaceful stream. These are just natural resources waiting to be exploited. This foolish attitude is not only exhibited toward other species, but resentment and injustice are expressly manifest amongst their own kind.

The naturally broad relational capacity of all human beings, the very source of their own existence, is reduced to the sphere of the measurable and the material. In this way, the invisible world and that of the sacred and wild presences that make available a life full of value, meaning, and consciousness, is effectively beyond reach.

The pain felt by the forest keepers is more than their small bodies are able to withstand. The little ones seek help. The chubby keepers, with hearts broken open after witnessing first-hand their brothers and sisters being slaughtered by the hand of greed and confusion, directly address the infinite source of wellbeing, love, and wisdom—Great Mother Earth.

Taking off their red hats in a sign of respect and admiration, the chubby beings gather all their fervor and loving intention to intercede before the Great Mother.

"Great Mother, we call upon you. Great Mother, we invoke you. Great Mother, help us. Assist our human brothers and sisters in recovering their memory. Help them listen once more. Great Mother, we ask for your loving presence to manifest in the minds and hearts of our fellow humans.

Great Mother, now more than ever, we need you. Allow our human kin to remember their sacred and mysterious nature, which is but your own essence; eternally wild, compassionate, and free."

The Great Mother, aware of the precarious situation unraveled by the confused humans entranced in compulsive cycles of planetary import, responds with a gesture of heartfelt generosity felt in the very depths of the cosmos.

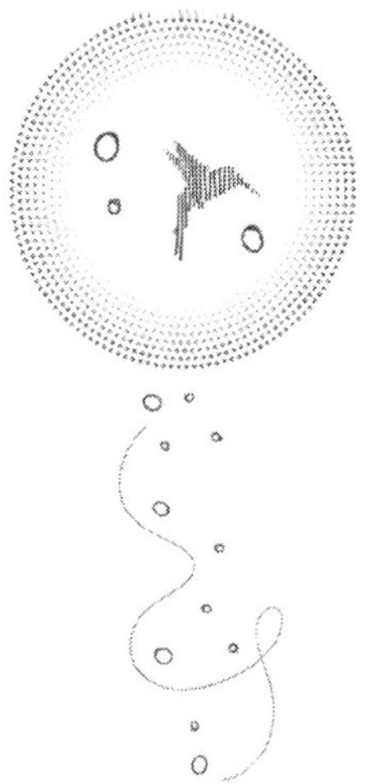

2.
ROUTINE AND CEMENT

Life passed at exorbitant speeds in the eyes of Artemio. Nothing in it seemed to invite change; everyday was but a carbon copy of the previous day. He felt like a passenger in the game of life, a passive observer of facts and situations whose cause was beyond his reach. The reason for things to be as they were was alien to him, as he irremediably considered it as something without importance or transcendence.

Artemio González, a 29-year-old business administration graduate, worked in a large Mexican metropolis—a country geologically located in North America, but with Central and South American soul. His work at a multinational developing firm with offices in his city kept him busy virtually every day of the week.

Artemio was undoubtedly a creature of routine. Most, if not all, his life's experiences seemed to adhere to the faithful adoption of repetitive practices, essential to maintaining his mental health. These habits ranged from blindly following society's dictates about his job, dress code, and way of thinking, all the way to keeping in mind the precise number of steps he climbed in a day and ringing the doorbell four times before entering his apartment.

He woke up early in the morning at the command of the alarm. From bed, he went straight to inspect his face with the aid of the bathroom's mirror. Once a series of unavoidable and terribly necessary actions had been carried out, he was ready to take a bath.

In a ritualistic manner, he then chose a combination of his many suits, ties, and shoes. By then, the intelligent coffeemaker had his coffee ready, which he poured into a thermos to drink on his way to work amidst slow-moving rows of cars. Sipping his coffee, he barely noticed the many background sounds of the urban landscape, muffled by the radio's hits of the moment.

After climbing 17 levels aboard a shiny elevator and cordially greeting his colleagues, Artemio arrived at his office to fulfill a full agenda of interviews, consultations, and deskwork. After a long day at the office, Artemio drove home always with the radio on—any constant noise served to keep his anxious mind occupied.

Back home, the first thing he did was turn the TV on in order to dispel the feeling of solitude that plagued his days. He truly believed that the voices coming from mindless TV shows kept him company. He'd then take off his suit, neatly hang it in its proper place in the closet, and immediately put on a heavy, fine robe inherited from his grandfather to easily move around in his apartment. Artemio felt quite uncomfortable when looking at his body.

After heating dinner in the microwave, he'd move to the living room to exclusively gift his attention to the TV screen. He was fond of sports and news shows because, according to him, they kept him in the loop and in touch with other people and society at large.

He often fell asleep on the sofa with the remote in his hand and a pile of frustrated dreams spinning around in his head. Panic attacks frequently woke him up in the middle of the night. He'd then go to his bed to negotiate some more sleep until the sound of the alarm announced the beginning of a new day.

Artemio navigated his life whilst counting steps, watching news shows, eating fast food, and religiously tending to his consuming job. In the eyes of his family and a few friends that he hardly ever saw, everything was OK. He fulfilled his role in society and had a steady job that provided enough money to lead a somewhat successful life.

Nevertheless, Artemio was secretly frustrated and unhappy, repeatedly questioning his own life. He often felt terribly uncomfortable while sitting in his office chair; his shirt collar stifled him, troubled by a nagging feeling of being trapped in his own clothes. A recurring felt-sense about the superficiality and futility of his deeds haunted him, which expressed as acute self-preoccupation and an accompanying avalanche of doubts and insecurities.

The only antidote to the rather demanding self-preoccupation episodes took the form of his childhood memories, particularly his family trips to the beach. Back then, he felt full and happy, filled with a peaceful sense of ease. He would walk along the beach in long quests for shells or some other sign of the inhabitants of those places. Or he would bathe and enjoy the warm waters of the Pacific Ocean for hours at a time, amused with the swaying of the waves.

At that time, his whole world distilled life and creativity, and everything—the beach sand, the palm trees, the ocean—spoke to him and conveyed its innermost secrets.

Little Artemio was prone to share his fantastic adventures in nature with his loved ones. One day, his father scolded him in front of a group of acquaintances for talking nonsense about the messages that the trees in the nearest park had entrusted to him.

From that point on, Artemio gradually stopped sharing about his adventures. The little one came to lose his special connection with the things around him, to the point where, years later, the mystery of life and the wild voices of nature were deeply buried in the desolate landscape of oblivion.

Such forgetfulness did not succeed in taking away the great peace he felt to this day in wild, open places. However, his busy schedule rarely allowed him to visit nature.

At times, his existential discomfort was followed by inexplicable moments of stillness and inner silence. Artemio felt that, in such moments, he floated like a disembodied presence with no purpose or end beyond just being. Just as they started, these placid yet eerie experiences of stillness abruptly came to an end. And again, he'd found himself observing the gray walls of his office.

Artemio had long been obsessed with cement, that gray material that seemed to cover everything around him in its different presentations and combinations. In his research, he had puzzlingly discovered that cement was made from natural elements, like those found in his favorite places of old.

Considering its origins, he could not comprehend how cement had such a cold and boring appearance. In fact, Artemio came to think that cement was the cause of his panic attacks. No matter how hard he tried, he couldn't get rid of both cement and anxiety. Cement seemed to own every last bit of his life.

Artemio thought to himself that if he'd be hard-pressed to describe what his life was like, he would say that it was grey, rigid, and cold. Just like cement. These adjectives equally applied to the people around him.

He believed that cement somehow passed on its properties to the people that surrounded it. It was as if cement charged a toll for all the services rendered to human beings, prompting certain habits and patterns of behavior.

Consequently, in Artemio's mind, cement influenced people's way of being, making them square and cold, almost machine-like. Perhaps that was the reason why people habitually refused to look into each other's eyes—their furtive glances unable to avoid the captivating magnetism of the grey compound underneath their feet and around them. Artemio felt rather strange and uncomfortable amongst cement-lovers and members of his own race.

His work had kept him so busy for the past eight years that he rarely left the city's concrete jungle. All this time had passed in the blink of an eye. In the last handful of years, he had managed to visit a couple of parks near his apartment that gave testament to the last green remnants in the city.

Like a cracked concrete block, Artemio felt that most people were split inside. He believed that, sometimes, he could even see the dark cracks that ran through the length and breadth of people, as a pattern either overlaid on, or within, their bodies.

Of course, this sense of fragmentation came from his own experience. The inner fracture accompanied him everywhere and in everything he did, felt, and thought. Artemio felt broken.

To the "human crack," as he called it, he attributed his lapses of physical and mental discomfort, as well as his lack of tolerance for silence and scarce patience toward others.

He was convinced that the abundance of grey and cold buildings and the consequent shrinking of places where human and more-than-human life could flourish freely was closely related to his sense of fragmentation and separation.

Broken and alienated from the world, Artemio went on with his life, treasuring the old memories of the wild places where he once felt so free, so complete.

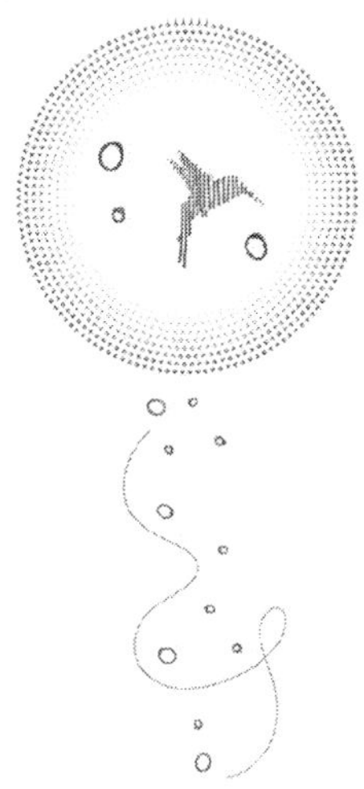

3.
CHRONICLES OF THE BLOOMING EARTH

"The story I am about to tell you is found in every cell of your being, spelled out in the innermost chambers of your heart."

Thus, began that voice, that penetrating and familiar sound that makes itself present in moments of stillness and peace, seemingly surfacing from the very depths of being.

Artemio was gripped by the sound of such a peculiar voice, while his conscious awareness, equipped with a combination of attentiveness and urgency, inhabited the intermediate realm between dreams and waking life.

Artemio saw himself sitting comfortably on a solid wooden bench in what appeared to be an old barn. The barn consisted of rows of long wooden benches, similar to those found in churches, arranged in concentric circles. At the center, there was a large, cube-like stone with unintelligible markings on its four sides.

Looking up, Artemio noticed that right above the central stone there was an opening of considerable size through which the starry sky could be seen. The moonlight enveloped the central area of the precinct, giving the peculiar stone and its surroundings a unique glow.

At Artemio's right side, there was a person that seemed quite familiar to him, yet he was unsure as to where he knew him from. He was a thin man wearing simple clothes and a straw hat. Without further ado, the man presented himself as Nool.

Nool, taking off the hat that left his silky hair uncovered, took a seat next to Artemio. In doing so, he amicably extended his arm and placed his hand on Artemio's knee, exerting considerable pressure.

It was as if Nool's hand helped keep Artemio in his seat. Otherwise he would fly aimlessly through the central opening beyond the barn. Then Nool began to speak:

"The story tells us that planet Earth emerged from the eternal bosom of the vast and kind Absolute. As a powerful and primordial presence, the Earth came into being as a generous source of life, hosting both material and subtle beings—gods, mortals, and demons alike. Her womb gave birth to the deities that dwell in the heavens, oceans, mountains, hells, and every living being you've had the pleasure of encountering, including your fellow humans."

Artemio realized that Nool's hand indeed served as an anchor to keep him in place. He was strangely pleased with himself. Perhaps due to the fact that, curiously, he felt more awake than in his everyday life.

"The birth of the planet originated in a tremendous explosion of love, a "big bang" that shook the very confines of this mysterious existence," Nool continued.

"This monumental outburst created a great cloud of dust and cosmic gases, setting in motion the spiral of time that allows for an evolving universe. The ever-present energy that feeds all began to coalesce into specific configurations amidst the expanding stellar cloud. One of these was giving birth to cosmic configurations such as the Milky Way galaxy, of which planet Earth is a very small part.

The Earth, as an evolving outgrowth of the original love-burst, serves as the immediate, generous matrix that allows our existence, always quenching the needs of Her many children. This is the reason why Earth's spirit has been praised and revered since time immemorial by different cultures as a Great Mother.

Tonantzin, Pachamama, Devi, Gaia, Pele, Onuava, Isis, Ala, Anu, Brigantia, Khon-Ma, Tara, Papatuanuku, Jord: all of them personifications of the great spirit and living body of the Earth. Thanks to Her and through Her, the divine cosmic mother, humans and all Earthlings are able to participate in the adventure of embodied existence."

Artemio had heard this story before, perhaps in school classes that spoke of world cultures that he had reluctantly attended. Be that as it may, and probably because of the influence of the dream realm, the story claimed a prominent place in his mind, allowing him for the first time to entertain the idea that the story was something more than an age-old fantasy.

Artemio looked up and examined the moon. It was in its growing phase, and its metallic light seemed to invite him to travel toward it.

"Our ancestors also conceived of the moon as a great goddess," Nool continued. "The Greeks called her Selene, the Maya refer to her as Ixchel, and the Lakota of North America know her as Hanwi. Her great beauty is a faithful companion of the Earth, and She is in charge of setting in motion the oceans and all planetary waters."

"Perhaps the waters of the Earth feel the same attraction for the moon as the one I feel for it now," Artemio thought to himself.

Artemio turned his attention to the floor of the barn. Up until then he hadn't realized that his bare feet were in direct contact with the damp, dark soil below. He realized that this too, the cool soil, was a tangible expression of the Great Mother, pregnant with creativity and always prepared to provide sustenance and shelter.

"The Earth's living body is approximately five billion years old," said Nool as he moved his legs into a more comfortable position.

Artemio's face betrayed his efforts to try to imagine such a gigantic time scale.

"I know that that figure is overwhelmingly large. Nevertheless, I'd like to invite you to make an effort to expand your mind and travel through the great spiral flow of geological and cosmic time. Keep in mind that not everyone revolves around our little conception of time and reality."

That last comment touched certain fibers in Artemio that made him somewhat uncomfortable. Even so, he acted as if nothing had happened.

"At first, the Earth was at very high temperatures and was dancing speedily around Her central star, the Sun. At every moment, Her body was bombarded by lightning, meteorites, and various particles from outer space.

The bowels of Earth's body were so hot that volcanoes, active at all times, served as an escape valve to Her unending heat. These were times of rapid change."

"How do you know all this, Nool?" Nool smiled slightly and continued with his story.

"Up in the sky, a dense layer of overheated gases accumulated, which became the respiratory system of the planet, the atmosphere. Meanwhile, rivers of magma rose from the depths and flowed constantly.

Gradually, temperatures mellowed. This allowed the rocky layer of the planet to take on a more fixed and definite form. The process of global cooling triggered a storm of apocalyptic dimensions that bathed and flooded the planet for thousands and thousands of years."

The storm reminded Artemio of the great flood, in which, according to Abrahamic traditions, Noah built an ark to safeguard the future of all beings. He was about to give voice to his thoughts, when Nool continued with his story.

"At that time, there was no expression of life as we know it today. But soon this would change.

The great storm gave rise to rivers, lakes, and lagoons in the highlands and to the vast oceans in the lowlands—planetary blood. The stage was set for the appearance of organic life.

Throughout time, countless humans have broken their heads trying to solve the riddle of life's origin. Perhaps it happened gradually or at the blink of an eye, or maybe the seeds of life traveled from outer space or someone or something planted them here.

I understand the curiosity quite well. The inquisitive mind is an intrinsic and beautiful capacity of the human species. But I won't be the one to answer such a transcendent question. At least not for now. That kind of knowledge is revealed to organisms that exist, let us say, more in tune with the great cosmic flow.

Knowledge of the origin of life in the hands of most humans today would translate into the end of their species. It would be like giving a machine-gun to a teenager while in a tantrum.

Suffice to say that life, once manifested in its material form, added to the planet a dimension of depth and complexity never experienced before. Life emerged, and the microscopic pioneering organisms distributed along the planet."

"Are the beings you speak of microbes?" asked Artemio in amazement.

"That's correct. Those admirable organisms that are invisible to the naked eye and erroneously feared by society.

The invisible has always caused both terror and fascination. Imagine your loved ones getting sick and dying from invisible agents and not having the slightest idea of why, as happened in ancient times.

This association between disease, death, and the bacterial family is strongly rooted in the human mind, bypassing entirely that a healthy human body is made up of trillions of these organisms. The human being is an ecosystem that carries within it the history of life and the signature of the whole cosmos. But let us return to our history.

There came a time when the creativity of the little pioneering beings enveloped the entire planet," continued Nool, widening his arms as if wanting to touch the horizon. "From the proliferation and convergence of unicellular organisms, more complex and differentiated beings emerged approximately 2 billion years ago, setting the stage for the diverse web of life that characterizes the planet.

Communities of winged beings, algae, fungi, reptiles, plants, mammals; all of them and many more, exist in constant expansion and contraction, coming and going, as if following the beating of Earth's heart.

The pulsating creativity of the planet surprises itself time and time again through its prodigious expressions. Of the many wonders of Earth's unfolding, I would like to focus on one in particular." This comment made Artemio's attention even sharper and more focused.

"Imagine the planetary jolt when, for the first time, beauty appeared in the form of a flower; a water lily very much like those that exist today."

"So, a lily is the father/mother of all flowering plants?" Artemio asked.

"Indeed," replied Nool.

"The emergence of the ancestral water lily had a dramatic effect on the ecosystems and climate of 180 million years ago, leading to the great success and distribution of flowering plants to the present day. The planet smiles in flowers," confessed Nool with a gentle smile.

"The human chapter amidst the unfolding creativity of the Earth is a tiny occurrence connected to an uninterrupted lineage of life and virtue. With the birth of the planet five billion years ago, it was only about three hundred thousand years ago that the human species emerged, once the dominion of the great reptiles came to an end.

By way of microbes, flowers, and reptiles, stardust made its way to human form, which allowed the primeval stellar energies to influence the entire planet in the last few centuries."

Stunned by the story, Artemio struggled to find the right words to convey the profound mixture of longing, sadness, and joy that seized him.

Nool, as if aware of Artemio's inner movements, looked at him with particular kindness. His eyes reflected the magnetic light of the moon when he asked Artemio, with the tenderness of a caring father addressing his son:

"Tell me, Artemio. In light of the ceaseless planetary vitality and uninterrupted cosmic creativity, how do we make of our lives a poem in the name of the flower's beauty?"

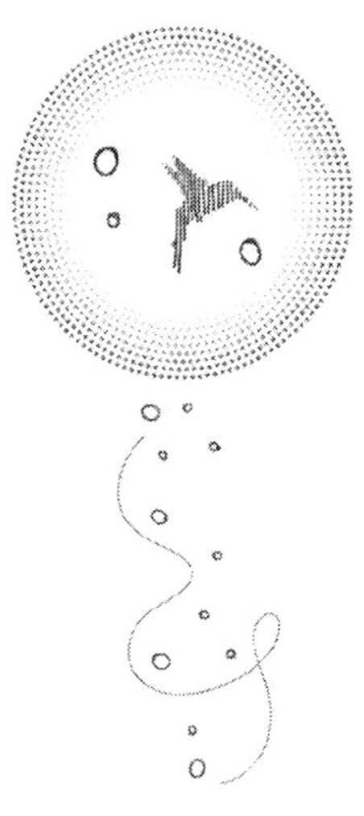

4.

COUNCIL OF ALL BEINGS

It was the crack of dawn in a tropical dry jungle off the Pacific coast of Mexico. The grey sky mutated into tones of purple, blue, and pink. There was a cool breeze coming from the ocean that whistled through the green leaves of the surrounding trees. It was the special day that marks the beginning of fall in the Northern Hemisphere, the autumn equinox; the time when day and night have equal duration.

There was a palpable sense of liveliness in the air, almost of hurriedness, due to the meeting that was about to take place. It was the largest gathering the bioregion had ever witnessed. In fact, there was no known precedent elsewhere for the magnitude of the event.

The attendees to the Council of All Beings, as the gathering was known, came from all of life's kingdoms with the explicit aim of addressing the ever-growing crisis threatening the planet.

This auspicious event, fruit of the request of the forest keepers and other Earth guardians, took place within a lush ravine surrounded by steep hills that turned and twisted in various directions. Such seclusion contributed to the locale's holy and wild appeal.

In addition, the ravine was graced by the presence of a stream that meandered through the lower parts. Flowing freely and steadily, the banks of the stream served as a meeting point for a great variety of beings.

The green iguana chatted with a small, green frog, endemic to the region, about the loss of ponds and streams in the area, while the nine-banded armadillo nodded in agreement with its pointed head.

The papaya tree invited the green macaw to taste one of its many ripe and sweet fruits, an offer that the macaw couldn't refuse. The common opossum, one of the few marsupials living outside the Australian continent, shared some of its favorite hangout spots with a long, thorny columnar cactus, emphasizing the regrettable increase of landfills in the area.

A few feet away the cincuate, or bull snake, patiently waited rolled up by the side of the stream, hypnotized by the oscillatory movements of the microorganisms that had gathered in the shallow waters.

Perched up on a tree's branch, the common vulture discussed the nutritional advantages of scavenging with an army of black ants, which had left the thorny Acacia tree they had as their home to attend the meeting.

These and many more creatures politely chatted with their neighbors while patiently waiting for the council's inauguration. The creatures were moved by a sincere interest in the welfare of their communities and a prosperous future for life on Earth.

Overall, there was a lively atmosphere, brimming with the diverse energy of the many beings present and the enormity of the challenges ahead.

The Sun rose behind the Eastern mountains, bathing them with a soft, warm light that dispersed its radiance throughout. That was the signal that the elder white-tailed deer and council facilitator, Kauyumari, was waiting to announce the beginning of the meeting.

Feeling the warm rays of sunshine on his face, Kauyumari stood on his hind legs and, placing his front legs on a segment of rock that served as a podium, cleared his throat a couple of times to attract the attention of the participants.

Almost immediately, the many voices faded. Only the wind's hissing through the foliage and the stream's murmuring prevailed. Kauyumari began:

"Dear comrades, I offer you a warm welcome to this your Council of All Beings." The attendants nodded in unison to the words of the old deer.

"I'd like to express my deep appreciation for each and every one of you, and apologize for the short notice given for the council. But, as we all know, the dire situation requires our immediate attention."

The community in attendance unreservedly had the utmost respect for Kauyumari. His reputation as a wise, experienced, and compassionate leader was not in vain. His voice was strong and soft at the same time. His movements unhurried but steady. His stance and overall demeanor conveyed a contagious sense of honesty and solidarity.

To the best knowledge of the attendees, there was no better person than the sage deer for the monumental task of containing and channeling the energy and reflections of the council. Kauyumari continued:

"We are here to enter into dialogue about the severe crisis we are now experiencing. We will focus our attention on the accelerated rate that our community is disappearing and the growing erosion of the values that guide a good life.

As we are well aware, this appalling situation has its origin in the activities of our human brothers and sisters, informed by their seemingly endless thirst for power and their myopic actions that lead to the destruction of us all.

We are here on this beautiful day in representation of the countless expressions of planetary clans, seeking to further the timeless dream of the Earth. We aim to keep nurturing this waking dream in our unique ways by tending the delicate balance between the worlds on which the fullness and realization of all beings depends upon.

We are gathered here today to celebrate life and the opportunities, challenges, and mysteries it offers us as proof of the resolve and courage needed to face the monumental crisis.

Today, we will share our feelings, thoughts, and experiences with an open heart in order to move ahead in graceful, life-honoring ways."

Quispe, the large basaltic boulder placed behind Kauyumari, asked to speak.

The wise deer gave way to Quispe's participation, presenting him as an ancient inhabitant of the region who would surely enrich the council with his long-range perspective and geological experience.

"Good morning dear friends," began Quispe with his deep, guttural voice that seemed to emanate from the entrails of the Earth. Rather than listening with their ears, the many beings perceived the voice of the ancient rock as a vibration in the middle part of their bodies.

"I will share with you a little of my life, directly related to the history of this place so we can properly honor and offer our respect to the beautiful landscape that welcomes us.

This is a special region because it is the meeting place of three mountain ranges. My body is made of the first basaltic lavas that were expelled by the youngest of these mountain ranges, which, in fact, is a belt of active volcanoes.

Newly arrived in the atmosphere from the sweltering depths, I was suppler and more mobile so was able to travel at considerable speeds. With the help of winds and rains, I found my way to where I am today. Once here, my body quickly hardened and began to take the oval shape that you're now witnessing."

Amazed, the participants of the council discovered that even rocks enjoy movement.

"Yes, rocks are able to travel the length and breadth of the planet, unless we return to the fiery Earthly bosom to then surface once again. It is largely due to our passing over the surface of the planet that there's soil to serve as the foundation for all terrestrial creatures.

Even mountains and volcanoes move. These ancient beings dance to the rhythm of underground tectonic movements, but their slow pilgrimage and large size make their movements difficult to perceive. Let's say their dance happens in deep time. When they increase their pace, they cause, for example, earthquakes and volcanic eruptions.

The area in which we find ourselves and the continent we inhabit are constantly changing. For instance, about 10 million years ago, segments of land began to emerge from the oceans, which later ended up connecting the North of the Americas with the South."

"This encounter and integration of life's kingdoms continues to nourish the collective consciousness of the inhabitants of this rich continent," said Kauyumari.

"The unification of the Americas gave way to a fruitful exchange of life," Quispe continued. "The fresh terrestrial formations kept pushing up to the sky, so as to form the great American mountain range, the backbone of the continent.

This true grandfather "apu" or mountain spirit is in charge of connecting and channeling the energy of the entire continent through different places of power distributed throughout mountain ranges of the three Americas."

"Could you please stop beating around the bush?" expressed Pili, the tick, with her high-pitched voice that revealed her growing enthusiasm.

Quispe didn't flinch in the slightest, but took the comment as a sign of the group's overall state.

"Good. It is necessary to offer our respect to these great movements, as they contribute enormously to forging our identity. Nature's long journeys are at the core our own beings, of our spirits. This long view helps us become acquainted with who we are, and sheds light on where we come from.

The movements and trajectories of the Earth influence our moods, our ways of thinking, our customs, and habits. Without the awareness of Earth's presence, without this sweeping perspective, our roots are easily cut off and our identity as offspring of sky and land is easily forgotten."

Suspended in the air for a few moments, Melina, the wide-billed hummingbird, thanked the apus of the surrounding mountains for granting their blessing and allowing the Council of All Beings to take place.

"As you can see, I am an old witness and active part of the great changes that this landscape, this bioregion, and our community have undergone," Quispe continued with his guttural voice.

"All of this doesn't compare with what we are experiencing today. The present period has been more dynamic, or to be precise, more destructive, than many past episodes of great change. Humans have managed to alter each and every ecosystem on the planet, overcoming even the ancestral geological forces of my lineages."

This comment caused a stir in the council. Attendees expressed their agreement in a chorus of squawks, roars, snorts, grunts, and howls, followed by a lively exchange among those present.

"That is true, but that twisted behavior does not apply to the entire human race," Kauyumari interceded with a calm yet penetrating voice. The comment brought silence back to the council.

The elder deer's eyes flickered with light, and his body emanated a subtle and calming bluish glow.

"Truly, some of our self-centered human brothers and sisters are terribly confused. Tell us Quispe, what virtues would you like to share with our deluded human kin?"

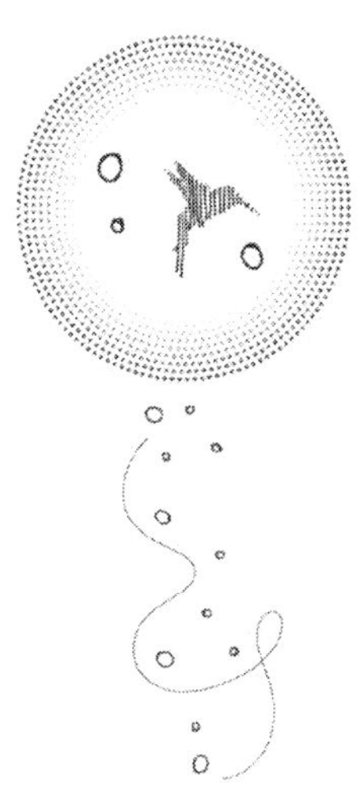

5.
REUNION

On a cloudy, windy day, Artemio's life took a 180-degree turn. The repetitive nature of his everyday life came to a halt when one of his periods of existential discomfort and weightlessness was so intense that he fell from his chair in a loud crash.

Co-workers in the adjoining cubicles quickly became aware of the situation. Meanwhile, Artemio lay on the floor babbling incoherently. Alarmed and not knowing what to do, his colleagues paced anxiously. A couple of them began to pray.

A few minutes went by that seemed like hours. Karen, from the neighboring cubicle, mustered all her courage to slowly approach Artemio's stiff body that was lying on the floor.

Just as she was about to touch Artemio, he stood up in one jolt, still babbling gibberish. Seconds later, he returned to his desk as if on autopilot. This surprised his co-workers even more.

By then, the floor manager had arrived at the scene. He politely asked Artemio to get up from his chair and, firmly holding his arm like someone who's helping a drunk friend, led him to his office.

Once behind closed doors, Artemio's boss described the reasons why, unfortunately, he could no longer work for the company. The speech boiled down to the fact that, although Artemio was a good employee, his behavior put the firm's image at risk. He had become a liability.

Artemio left the floor manager's office still disoriented. It was as if an invisible haze around him prevented his attention to focus on any particular thing. He managed to quickly return to his office, followed by the disapproving stares of the staff as he walked down the aisle. He dropped to his chair to look at the gray cement around him for the last time.

Artemio rejoiced at the thought that he would never again be surrounded by the coldness of those walls. He packed the few belongings on his desk and headed for his car. As he turned it on, he recognized a long-forgotten sensation, he didn't know what the future had in store for him.

Without planning it, Artemio had freed himself from the heavy shackles of his boring and tediously calculated life. He drove for hours with no fixed destination, until the fuel gauge came dangerously close to empty.

He finally made it home. Feeling an unusual inspiration, he evaded his favorite armchair in front of the television to cook a hefty dinner with surprising dedication, using some leftovers he found in the fridge. When he finished savoring his food, he fell into a deep sleep.

The ringing sound of his cell phone woke Artemio the next morning. To his great surprise, it was José Velázquez, a lifelong friend with whom he had lost contact several years back due to work. José called to invite him on one of his nature expeditions. Without further ado, Artemio agreed.

***

Several days passed in which Artemio and José explored and enjoyed the jungle. They were making the last preparations to return to the nearest town and placate their hunger at the first food stall in sight.

Sitting, attempting to free himself from his stiff, heavy boots, Artemio became aware of a strange but remotely familiar sensation.

He stood up and, with his bare feet in direct contact with the Earth, paid close attention to his surroundings.

He found the landscape so beautiful and touching that he just stood there, in silent awe and wonder. The trees, the birds' song, the gentle passing of clouds above, the varied shades of green all around—everything, somehow, seemed different. Same but different. It was as if a native child lent her eyes to Artemio to contemplate the landscape in a fresh, renewed way.

His body was showered with feelings of belonging, happiness, and fullness. Artemio turned in José's direction, looking for a sign that he too experienced a similar state of being. He did not have to vocalize his question, as he almost immediately felt a "no" answer in the middle of his body.

Then, the sensation around his belly turned into a kind of urgency that gave way to a clear conviction: he had to return to the depths of the jungle.

He put on his boots and told José to go ahead into town, as he would return to the jungle. José looked at him puzzled, but only shook his head approvingly, given Artemio's soft, yet convincing determination.

Artemio made his way back into the jungle, without any particular destination in mind. It was as if his body knew exactly where he was going. He trusted this fleshy guidance and gave himself to the experience.

After a while, Artemio arrived at the base of a charming ravine in the entrails of the jungle. He had no idea how long he had walked, but it must have been a considerable time since he was drenched in sweat. It was a somewhat humid place, populated by tall, leafy trees with stylized curled lianas. There was a gentle stream a few steps away. He reached his hands in and poured some water on his face and neck to refresh himself.

Lying on the ground beside the stream, he heard strange noises upstream. A great curiosity invaded him, and he began walking toward the place where the sounds came from.

After a few minutes walking uphill following the stream, he turned right and found a rather peculiar, dream-like scene—it was the Council of All Beings! Such was the impression of the extravagant vision that Artemio's rational functions were not even able to take the reins and intercede.

Kauyumari, the elder deer, approached him and greeted him profusely, saying that he was very grateful and honored by his presence.

"Please sit down, make yourself comfortable," Kauyumari continued in order to reassure him.

"We were just talking about you and your friends a few moments ago," Quispe commented. "In fact, we are quite interested in the activities of your kin and their impacts on our home."

"We are very concerned about the destructive behavior of your species, so we asked the Wild Spirit to lead a human to our council to consider your people's point of view," said Kauyumari. "But it was up to you to heed the call and come here today. And so, you did," the elder deer added, smiling broadly.

"Today, on this auspicious day marked by the equanimity and balance of the equinox, we are holding the largest multi-species meeting ever held to reflect on the historic moment of crisis the planet is undergoing."

Artemio did not know what to say. A whirlwind of feelings seized him. From within the inner whirlwind, a mixture of sadness, anger, and shame made itself apparent.

Kauyumari turned to the sky and stared for a long time, as if looking for something. Time seemed to pass by differently for Artemio. All the participants remained silent while Kauyumari gazed into the sky. He fixed his attention on a cluster of clouds on their gentle, westward journey through the bright blue sky.

Then, lowering his head, the wise deer focused his attention on the surrounding jungle. His eyes twinkled and the bluish glow that the participants had previously witnessed around his body appeared again.

Artemio looked directly at Kauyumari. He felt flooded by the sparkling blue glow, allowing him to gain a deepened sense of connection to the ravine and the jungle. He could feel the nearby stream like a fresh current traveling up and down his spine, the copal tree's presence lured him to enter the corridors of deep time, while the collective intelligence of the ants expressed as a constant tickle at the crown of his head.

Artemio was able to feel what "the other" felt. It was as if his skin was the air that penetrated and enveloped the entire jungle. His sense of space and time collapsed, which caused the tingling at the crown of his head to distribute throughout his body.

The jungle and Artemio joined into a single organism. Then, he just knew in great detail what the council participants had been sharing.

Soon after, the jungle and the participants of the council transformed into a network of snakes of light that intertwined in all directions while dancing with undulating movements. The astonishing vision was accompanied by a peaceful feeling of warmth and tenderness.

In the midst of it all, Artemio managed to perceive a tangle of bluish filaments traveling directly toward him. The bluish glow devoured him. The experience was just too much. Artemio fainted.

When he came to, Artemio found himself lying on the ground. He was not sure if minutes or months had passed. Kauyumari approached. After carefully inspecting him, as if sweeping Artemio's body with his gaze, the deer announced that all was well and made him sit down.

"You are certainly welcome here," Kauyumari continued once Artemio regained some composure. "We could all benefit from your presence here in our Council of All Beings."

These words worked as an antidote. Artemio remembered what had happened. He felt renewed and light, but with a clear sense of being split in an indefinite part of his being. The longing to become whole filled his eyes with tears.

Artemio couldn't help but turn his attention to the causes of the severe planetary impasse and why he and the so-called civilized members of his own species seemed out of tune with the rest of creation.

Moments later, Quispe, addressed Artemio, who felt the ancestral rock's voice like a cavernous vibration that echoed in his chest.

"Artemio, from now on you can draw nourishment from the ancient support and sustenance of the mineral kingdom. The patience and perseverance of the rock are yours, as is the strength to resist the onslaughts of those who act against life's integrity. The portal that connects with the memory of ancient time is now within your reach. We are with you."

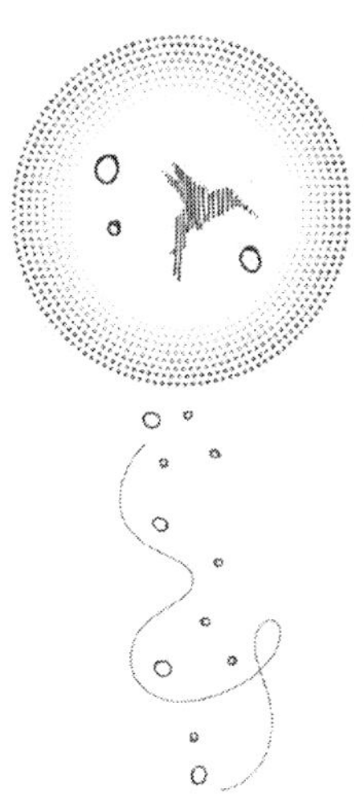

6.
THE SPELL OF THE MACHINE WORLD

The council participants had assimilated Artemio's presence as one more member of the gathering. Among them, the largest feline in the Americas expressed his intention to share a few words.

"But of course. It would be a great honor," replied Kauyumari.

The different creatures were impressed with the appearance of the feline and the refined grace and extreme precision of his movements. Until that moment, Tuwe, the jaguar warrior, had remained lying on the ground, concealing his majestic presence.

Tuwe was two meters long (over 6 feet), had a massive head, sharp fangs, powerful legs, and an exquisite coat with dark patterns that resembled an ancient message engraved by the gods themselves. His eyes, in all their intensity, expressed his incorruptible will.

After finding a suitable place to sit, he emitted a series of roars and grunts that further captured the attention of those present. Then he began:

"There was a time when most human beings were intimately acquainted with the sacred powers of nature and the cosmos. While experiencing themselves as having defined limits inhabiting a solid and tangible reality, deep within they saw themselves as one of the many expressions of the invisible and infinite source, always exploring and finding ways to innovate and create in their unique ways.

Not only did they understand this apparent dichotomy, but they were a true embodiment of the all-pervasive, mysterious creativity. The Great Mystery impregnated their every act."

Before proceeding, Tuwe paused briefly, evaluating the effect of his words on the audience.

"These human brothers and sisters were fluid, kind beings capable of fantastic feats given that, as I mentioned earlier, they experienced as a living tendril of the wild and holy potentiality of the world, recreating itself at all times, in all places.

It is said that these people could shapeshift into any creature around them, given their intimate kinship with the creative force that animates everything from within. But perhaps their greatest feat was to keep the flame of peace and kindness burning in their hearts, as they actively tended to the dynamic balance of life's web."

Artemio moved nervously in his seat, while a pair of green macaws, placidly perched on a branch of the copal tree, swayed rhythmically from side to side.

"If we pay close attention, we can see that a fundamental truth that directed the life of these fine people was the unfathomable interdependence of the cosmos," Tuwe continued.

"The minds and hearts of these beings did not know of unconscious fragmentation, but actively nurtured and fed the network of precious relations at the core of creation.

Over time, however, the once celebrated knowledge of interdependence and intimate belonging was gradually forgotten and relegated only to certain members of the community.

The people I am referring to have been known by many names throughout time. Referred to as healers, seers, shamans, sorcerers, magicians, naguals, witches, and more, according to the historical context that welcomed them, they were forced to safeguard the precious interdependent wisdom in the inner precincts of the heart's temple."

"How come the ways of relational communion, reverence, and interdependence were forgotten?" asked Pili, the tick, somewhat alarmed.

"Excellent question," answered Tuwe.

"Although shrouded in mystery, it's known by sages and wisdom keepers that the root of the pervasive amnesia of the sacred is found in a powerful type of magic, known as the spell of the machine world."

At that precise moment, a gust of wind shook the surrounding trees. This brought a short-lived but definite shudder amongst the council participants.

"The spell of the machine world has proven extremely effective. Given its widespread effects, humans were impelled to manufacture all sorts of gadgets and tools in order to control nature. This magnified their already misguided sense of superiority, as they were increasingly capable of predicting and manipulating the world, a world destined to be exploited.

The penetrating effects of the spell on the collective mind cause people to unquestionably conceive the world as a machine, while the kinder, more reciprocal, and wakeful ways of being are, at best, relegated to the realm of legend and myth.

Perhaps the most serious effect of the spell is the emergence of a restricted sense of self, source of ceaseless suffering for humans and the rest of Earth's community. The confusion around who they truly are is not necessarily malignant, but it sets the stage for dreadful difficulties as the now domesticated human ignores its very essence."

The participants at the council felt as if a dark haze had enveloped their hearts. Many of them lamented quietly the predicament of the human condition, while others expressed a sincere sense of empathy and compassion.

"This ingrained, invisible structure within the human mind fosters violent and unconscious behaviors," said Tuwe, once again getting the attention of those present, faithfully following each of his words.

"Humans carry within their souls the enormous pain of disconnection. At the same time, they long to celebrate and honor their true essence as boundless beings in unbroken kinship with the source of all life.

The spell of the machine world breeds suffering, bounding humans to compulsive cycles of denial and confusion. The resulting existential crisis leads them to repress the difficult feelings about the harm systematically inflicted upon our common home.

The offspring of a fragmented state of being, this ignorance erodes the health and wellbeing of all of us, while normalizing the suicidal behaviors of our brothers and sisters."

Silence reigned for a long time at the council. Tuwe lay completely motionless. Eyes closed. He seemed to be in a state of deep meditation.

"How do you all feel?" Kauyumari asked in a soft voice that echoed through the ravine.

A mixture of tension and deep grief pervaded the air. Artemio was particularly gripped by it. The darkened haze that enveloped the participants' hearts contributed to worsening the young human's condition, taking him to the verge of a nervous breakdown. The sensation of being ruptured in an indefinite part of his being became acutely present.

Artemio fell to the ground, finding the comfort of the firm, fertile soil. At that precise moment, Tuwe opened his eyes to continue with his story.

"This jungle is not only shaped by a multitude of creatures, but the Wild Spirit itself bonds each and all of us through time and space. This holy unity provides our ultimate purpose in this life.

Bees and bats pollinate flowers; ants transfer nutrients and maintain a healthy balance by predating other insects; birds and mammals transport seeds that regenerate the forest; vultures and other scavengers contribute to the essential cycling of nutrients; termites recycle organic matter from the soil, making it available to plants.

When I go in search of my dinner, I might find one of my favorite foods—a solitary collared peccary. Similar to a pig, this mammal feeds on various roots and fruits, along with the tasty nuts of the cohune palm found throughout, all packed with the Sun's energy. This energy returns to the ecosystem by way of breath and feces, which in turn disperses seeds previously ingested throughout the jungle.

With care and stealth, I snatch the peccary and pierce its skull with my powerful fangs, to partake in the flows of energy needed to survive. I too contribute to transferring the life-giving energy made available to plants through the activities of scavengers and decomposers. The cycle is renewed.

The energy that gives life to the jungle dwells in all of us, including our human brothers and sisters. The Spirit of the jungle never dies."

"The Wild Spirit is far more powerful than the seemingly invincible spell of the machine world," intervened Kauyumari.

"The origins of this ancient Spirit are lost in the depths of the Absolute. All the fortitude, creativity, and love that existed from the origin of time dwell in the heart of the Great Mother. And Her precious heart beats within all beings. The Wild Spirit is unstoppable."

"The good news is that not all humans are trapped in the cobwebs of the machine world," the great feline added. "There are those who see through the wicked effects of the spell, inspired by glimpses of the Wild Spirit, vibrantly manifest in the holy, interdependent matrix of creation.

Despite the numbing onslaughts of machine wizardry, these brave human brethren refuse to denigrate the most precious thing that exists; life and its eternal flux.

Humans touched by the Wild Spirit's fierce kindness and generosity carry within them the strength of the Earth. Like human-salmon swimming upstream, their unyielding intention to oversee the wellbeing and integrity of their planetary relatives is rooted in their devotion to life.

It is with this kind of humans that my lineage, that of the great jaguar warrior, has been in direct contact since time immemorial. For the ancient inhabitants of Mesoamerica, for example, the jaguar is a powerful deity. We are the "heart of the mountain" that makes the Earth tremble. These peoples are well acquainted with the virtues of my lineage.

In honor of the timeless alliance between jaguar and human, I'd like to offer some of these gifts to our illustrious human guest."

The attention of the whole council turned to Artemio. Wobbling, the young man stood up and nervously managed to reach the center of the circle to sit.

Tuwe approached slowly and stopped at the precise distance to gently place his powerful right claw on Artemio's head. Tuwe's claw seemed to carry the weight of the world. His left claw lifted into the air like an antenna that picks up frequencies from the heavens. Then he began to speak.

"The primeval, yet ever-renewed Wild Spirit has blessed my lineage with agility, elegance, authority, and spiritual strength. For that, I'm truly grateful. Now, I'd like to bequest the mental agility and refined skill needed to go beyond the spell of the machine world. Artemio, may you embody the commanding presence of a great predator, aimed at everything that hinders the ancient flow of life.

The spiritual strength of the great jaguar warrior is the radiance that leads from destruction to harmony, from confusion to remembrance, from darkness to the new dawn.

From the heart temple, the jaguar's roar transmits the frequencies of light that restore the presence of the Wild Spirit in our everyday lives. Artemio, recognize now that the honorable spiritual strength of the jaguar clan resides always in your heart."

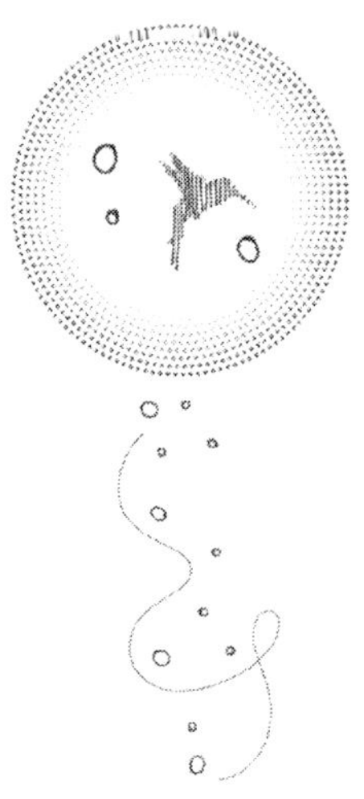

7.

BIRD'S-EYE VIEW

"I would like to know more about those humans who can see through the spell of the machine world," Artemio commented in a casual tone, but clearly revealing his keen interest in the topic.

"As Tuwe mentioned, these illustrious beings continually hoist the flag of peace to the heights of the heart-sky," Kauyumari, the sage deer and council's facilitator, answered cryptically.

"These caring human kin are guided by the covenant between the sacred origin and life's holy compost that continually renews all that exists toward its glorious destiny," continued the elder deer, deepening his already enigmatic commentary.

Looking around, Artemio learned that the many creatures around him thoroughly agreed with Kauyumari's words. The young human, for his part, could not penetrate their meaning.

"All in good time," expressed Kauyumari. Once again, the old deer seemed to be aware of what was taking place in Artemio's inner landscape.

"Now, we shall give our attention to Eshéni, the white-throated magpie."

“As we know, the spell of the machine world is entrenched in so-called civilized societies around the planet,” Eshéni began promptly, as her long bluish tail shook from side to side.

“The inner, self-sabotaging tendency responsible for so much havoc and suffering that Tuwe referred to is clearly active at a social scale. At this level, the spell of the machine world fuels the illusion of progress and endless growth in the name of profit.

The mandate of exponential profit at all costs serves as the guiding force of human activities. Our sisters and brothers live trapped in repetitive cycles of consumption and exploitation without even knowing it, all the while believing that the accumulation of things is tantamount to happiness and fulfillment. Addiction to instant gratification generates whole Earth suffering.”

“So, profit for the sake of it inevitably brings unchecked greed and destructive confusion?” asked Artemio, palpably saddened by the actions of his species.

This comment ensued due to Artemio’s endless days at the office. Maybe because the belief had been instilled in him since childhood, his ingenuous mind assumed that future success and personal fulfillment depended on the amount of money in his bank account and on blindly following societal dictates.

“Not necessarily Artemio,” replied Eshéni, relieving him from his ponderings.

“In essence, money is a kind of energy exchange. This poorly misunderstood concept becomes problematic when conceived as divorced from wild nature, as the final end of all human endeavor. The dilution of the great mystery of existence to a few coins; that is the problem.

The fixation on artificial money has created a global monoculture of mind that perpetually engenders voracious consumers with little or no discernment.

Rooted in the soil of consumption, the human monoculture is kept alive through the activities of financial institutions, mass media, international legislations, and a variety of tricks that pass on twisted ethical principles. These values make the world a massive storehouse of goods and resources available to the highest bidder.

I consider the Internet and television to be some of the most efficient technologies for inoculating beliefs, effectively becoming parental figures that lead human sheep around the globe along the hollow paths of craving and discontent."

"Eshéni, do you mean that people living in the next village or at the foothills of the Himalayan peaks or around the Atacama Desert are all subject to the same corporate, brain washing influence?" asked Petra, the opossum.

"That's right," replied Eshéni.

"They are systematically bombarded by separatist messages and deluded needs and ways of being. The spell of the machine world proficiently makes of humans a docile, malleable, and numbed out species. They become machine-like.

Machine-people are devoted to automated gadgets, often only having distant memories of what the world was like before plasma screens, cell phones or automobiles. The relationship of humans with machines has become an addictive, bizarre dependency.

But it's not all black and white. Media outlets, wireless technologies, and many other means of global communication are also used to nurture and celebrate the generosity of the Wild Spirit. The potential for positive change by respectfully using these technologies seems limitless."

Coming from an urban setting, this comment prompted Artemio to emit an audible sigh of relief.

"Yet the dominant system is corrupt at its core, perpetuating long-standing social diseases such as racism, classism, sexism, militarism, and patriarchal propensities that stifle life's free expression," continued Eshéni.

"The global monoculture is based on a twisted logic that enables the gluttony of the few at the expense of the many. It is nauseating. This logic results in social disparity and injustice, violence, homelessness, and much more. Meanwhile, the life support systems of the planet collapse."

The participants of the council followed Eshéni's remarks attentively. Artemio felt tremendous anger and hopelessness. Strangely, as he looked around, he realized that, although most creatures seemed to share a certain level of agitation, there was no trace of hatred or resentment in them.

"As offspring of the spell of the machine world, the global financial system has persuaded our human kin to conceive of living beings as things," Eshéni continued. "And things exist to be used up and discarded."

"Moreover, all these "things" are valued according to human needs. This means that every living creature that is not human is worth nothing in and of itself. Nature's worth, as I mentioned, is set by the mandate of profit at all costs.

As we know, this bigotry is well and alive even amidst members of their own species," intervened Ramón, the robust breadnut tree. "It seems that the so-called civilized humans cannot see beyond their own reflection, endlessly rippling through time and space. The resultant impalpable prison, full of "I, me, mine," is made manifest by the predatory economic system."

Silence reigned for some time. The gentle hiss of the wind allowed the council participants to further reflect on the human-planet predicament.

"I would like to share with you just one more effect of the global monoculture and its ailments," continued Eshéni with a solemn voice. A crisp sadness was evident in her eyes.

"Civilized humans believe that their particular way of expression and communication is unique. At best, they believe that the many languages and voices of nature serve only the purpose of improving our chances of survival in the midst of the fierce fight of evolution."

The whole council found Eshéni's comment hilarious. A roar of laughter echoed through the ravine, well beyond the location of the council. Petra, the opossum, found the remark particularly absurd, as she chocked with laughter rolling on the ground.

Finally, Petra sat down. Between her outbursts of laughter, she managed to speak:

"How could we have this gathering? How could we even live?"

Her comments caused a second upsurge of communal laughter; a wild chorus composed of the most diverse tones and rich sounds.

"How did domesticated humans come to see themselves as so special and unlike everyone else?" asked Petra once she regained her composure.

"That's a great question with a complex answer," Eshéni replied. "Suffice it to say here that, in relation to language, humans previously "read" first-hand value and meaning in birds' flight, the positioning of the Sun, the scents of a nearby river or the cyclical passing of the seasons. Language was nurtured by such natural occurrences. Communication was more fluid and inclusive.

This pervasive meaning that allowed open, multi-species communication was then relegated to manuscripts filled with human-made symbols. For a time, books were precious repositories of knowledge, and as such have been the source of countless battles, advancements, and revolutions.

Value and meaning have been shrinking ever since, replaced by the self-centered monologues of our human kin, fervently attached to their own creations. Thus, the reciprocity between humans, landscape, and the Wild Spirit was muted.

With this I'd like to highlight that the lack of communication between humans and the chorus of voices of this magnificent planet is a fundamental cause of the severe crisis we're facing."

"How do you feel about all this?" asked Eshéni, as she looked around with curiosity. The gathering emitted a sustained humming sound in full agreement.

"Thank you kindly for your valuable comments," said Kauyumari. Eshéni's chest swelled disproportionately, to the extent that it seemed about to burst.

"I would like to ask you, without feeling you need to, if you'd like to pass on any gifts to Artemio, our human guest." Kauyumari continued.

Closing her eyes for a few moments, Eshéni subtly nodded affirmatively.

"Artemio, it is my sincere honor to grant you the ability to consciously listen, ability that transcends longstanding beliefs of who or what deserves our attention. With this finely-tuned ear you will be able to hear once again the voices of wild nature.

A refined ear is directly connected with an encompassing perspective, a bird's-eye view, that reveals patterns of connection and reciprocity even in the darkest of places. This standpoint will allow you to see through deeply ingrained cultural diseases and take rightful, compassionate action in service of reconciliation and healing. The sharp eye and acute listening capacity of the bird clan will always be with you."

Artemio remained in place, taking deep breaths, while copious tears streamed down his cheeks. One of these precious drops ran its course, throwing itself into the air and landing on the earth below.

At that very moment, Tuwe, the great jaguar warrior, stood up and became stiff as a rock. All his muscles and tendons were fully tensed, while attentively sniffing the air right above his head.

With the same agility and elegance, Tuwe relaxed his body and casually mentioned for everyone to remain alert, to prepare for the unexpected.

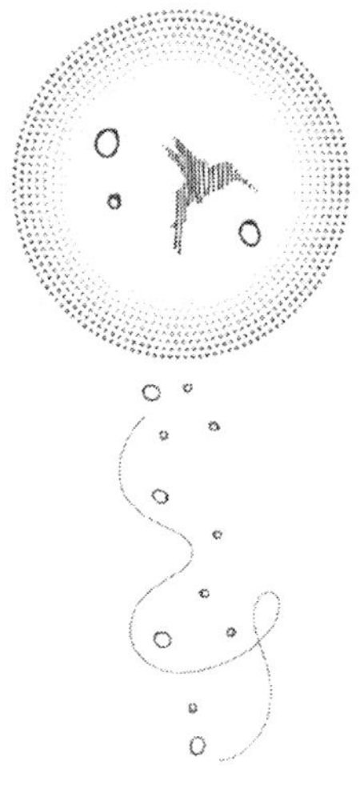

8.

ANCESTRAL MUTANT JUNGLE

"You know, colleagues, it's odd how humans focus their attention and select, so to speak, what they want to see and what they don't. Our home, the tropical dry jungle, is a good example of this," began Tonalli, the resilient copal tree.

"Humans have had a close bond with these jungles for thousands of years. This is the place where our human kin, inhabitants of the mistakenly named New World, evolved closely with plants such as corn, beans, and tomatoes, and animals like chickens and zebu, indispensable for their sustenance.

The tropical dry jungles have hosted great civilizations, including the Maya and the Mixtec. Together, humans and jungle have flourished through time."

At this point, Ramón, the breadnut tree, emphasized that he was a fundamental part of the Mayan diet, and that even today he was an abundant source of food for a wide variety of creatures.

"As Ramón rightly suggests, to this day, some native groups get about half of their food supply from tropical dry jungles," Tonalli continued.

"As a community, we are one with change. In the dry season, we turn into a brownish network that may give the impression of being devoid of life. But this is just an illusion. My tree family remains somewhat dormant and the overall rhythm of life decreases. Fallen leaves dry up, and insects, frogs, and many other creatures return to their quiet, cozy dwellings to get some rest.

When the rains come, they bring freshness and vibrant greenery. This is a time of radiant expression in which the trees and other plant beings grow their foliage, turning the landscape into a rich tapestry of green hues. Life thrives.

The rain wets the leaves accumulated on the ground where the micro-life awakens from its dry sleep. Meanwhile, there's a proliferation of lush flowers at the tree-top level that attracts various birds, bats, and small insects that serve as pollinators.

We embrace the whole of life's cycle. The presence or absence of water in our community has developed our remarkable capacity to adapt and flow in the face of change."

"Let us not be deceived by the name given to our home. The tropical dry jungle is not always dry. Rather, we are a mutant jungle," commented Kauyumari, the elder deer, laughing out loud at his own comment.

"I could not have expressed it better, my dear Kauyumari," replied Tonalli. Her response reflected the great affection Tonalli had for the wise deer.

"I would now like to address Artemio directly, and share some of what we have learned in the face of change."

Artemio, now feeling more at ease around the council's participants, made his way to the center of the circle to take a seat directly facing the blood-red copal tree.

Tonalli was robust and imposing. Her branches extended here and there, but always in an upward direction. With a height of about 25 meters (82 feet), her trunk was mostly straight. Her leaves, arranged in spirals, were of a bright green color. But what attracted Artemio's attention the most was the coppery bright red color of her trunk, which reminded him of the blood that animates his own people.

"Imagine my plant family endlessly complaining about the absence of water in the dry season. It doesn't make sense, does it?" Tonalli began.

"Instead, with fallen leaves, we learn to produce energy from our trunks and branches. Dropping our leaves also helps us retain the life-giving liquid within us for longer periods.

If we held off and disagreed with the changing times, we would simply die. The art of non-resistance is fundamental—the acceptance of things as they are. Sweet or bitter. Or bittersweet.

Be that as it may, the thorough acceptance of things goes beyond negativity and heaviness, and facilitates more harmonious, joyful, and wholesome ways of being. A wonderful thing is that the gifts of not being at odds with life not only benefit ourselves, but nurture all our relations.

By dropping our leaves, we favor the growth of some of our shorter relatives. Without much obstruction, sunlight penetrates the jungle's floor, allowing the little ones to produce their own food and grow.

As I said, accepting change releases enormous amounts of energy that are conducive to wellbeing, creativity, and joy. Being a mutant community means we're not weighed down by the nefarious heaviness of resentment when we disagree with how things are. We simply abide and accompany what is in the best possible way. We become one with change.

Smiling at life in this way nurtures the whole of life in its evolutionary journey. It is for this reason that the dry jungles of these regions are amongst the most diverse of their kind on the planet. We serve as home to a vast array of living beings, many of them only found here. Also, we're a temporary home for various organisms, including birds and bats that, on their seasonal pilgrimage, visit our jungles to seek shelter during the winter season.

As you can see, agreement at the heart level with the circumstances presented to us is a basic practice that connects us with the Wild Spirit. Do you understand what I mean, Artemio?"

Without giving him time to reply, Tonalli continued, flowing with the inspiration of the moment.

"If you pay close attention, the exercise of open-hearted acceptance entails trust. As the leaves of our branches fall, we could also fall into one of the many self-indulgent holes of blind fear. But this is not the case. We become even more rooted in the life force within us and in the mystery of existence that surrounds us.

We trust the Wild Spirit. We give ourselves to it. This is made possible by genuinely accepting change. This capacity exists within you too. It is yours, take it, and put it into practice from now on."

Artemio nodded affirmatively while keeping his eyes closed. As he opened them, he brought his right hand to his heart and was able to feel its constant beating, like a ceremonial drum.

"That's the rhythm that allows for radical acceptance to bless our lives," Kauyumari commented in a kind, fatherly tone.

Swiftly, the council's attention focused on Tonalli. From her trunk and branches emanated a fragrant white smoke.

As he tried to stand up, Artemio felt Kauyumari's soft but firm hoof over his right shoulder, inviting him to remain sitting.

"We know that vast tracts of dry tropical rainforest disappear at the hands of humans every year," continued Tonalli. "Not so long ago, we spread continuously throughout Central America. Now, where there was jungle there are cities, plantations, and pasture fields for various animals of human consumption.

"We also know that in the absence of dry jungles, the water cycle, the climate, and soil fertility are disrupted," intervened Ramón, the breadnut tree. "And of course, the quality of life of hundreds and thousands of living beings decreases to the detriment of all."

"Where there was jungle, now desolation reigns," continued Tonalli. "Where before the rhythmic songs of insects and birds embellished the Earth, there are now endless machine-made noises that emit hazardous vapors. This collective death occurs all over the planet, as you all know. It's a global tragedy.

Domesticated humans seem incapable of accepting their place in the natural order. This unfortunate occurrence has engendered within them harsh feelings of contempt toward nature, believing that the Earth Mother has turned Her back on them. Feeling orphaned and with a heart full of resentment, they declare war on the mother of all."

At this point, the white smoke surrounding Tonalli increased to form a long column connecting earth and sky, wide enough to envelop all council participants.

With its rich, earthy scents, the white smoke smudged the many beings, casting a spell of levity and protection. Artemio remained at the center of the circle.

"It is urgent that the industrial human awakens from the machine spell to reclaim its place in the natural order," said Ramón, the breadnut tree.

"One of the great antidotes to the confusion and resentment of orphanhood is to celebrate our indelible connection to our ancestors. After all, it is because of them that we are here," confessed Tonalli.

While Tonalli continued, her precious white smoke penetrated the innermost chambers of the participants' hearts, thoroughly cleansing and nourishing each and every beating fiber.

"The guidance and power of our ancestors, our families, our people, are made available by the practice of radical acceptance. This, in turn, allows us to live life more fully. By taking our ancestors into consideration and doing activities on their behalf, our lives extend through time, as we actively nourish the unbroken lineages that facilitate our existence. A sense of fellowship and belonging ensues when we recognize that, in a very real way, we are the result of all those that preceded us.

You, me, and everyone else are the offspring of the dreams and shortcomings of our ancestors. We are honorable members of a lineage of life that pulses with the same force that makes the Sun shine or the Earth spin. This ancient flow of compassionate wisdom connects us to the sacred, original source."

"Our bright ancestors are always ready to lend us a hand," Kauyumari contributed. To which he added:

"In order to restore the natural order, it is necessary to open our hearts and humbly come to terms with the fact that we are the fruit of the love of our ancestors."

Interwoven in the planet's bosom, the natural order takes us beyond delusions of either neglect or inflated importance to deliver us, just as we are, to our rightful place," said Tonalli. "It is from that place that we can access deep forgiveness. Forgiveness of what? We might ask.

Accepting things as they are calls for a patient, gentle recognition of the times in which we may have transgressed the natural order. No need for guilt, justifications, or complaints. Simply, we increase our responsibility, our becoming aware, bit by bit. This is how we honor and give praise for the gift of existence. Each time in a kinder, more wholesome, and more inclusive way.

This kind of forgiveness of oneself and others springs forth from a peaceful place within, populated by our ancestors, guides, and allies."

After some time, the healing white smoke of the copal tree completely vanished. Artemio felt once more the weight of Kauyumari's hoof on his shoulder. This time, it was to invite him to stand up and return to his place in the circle to continue with the council.

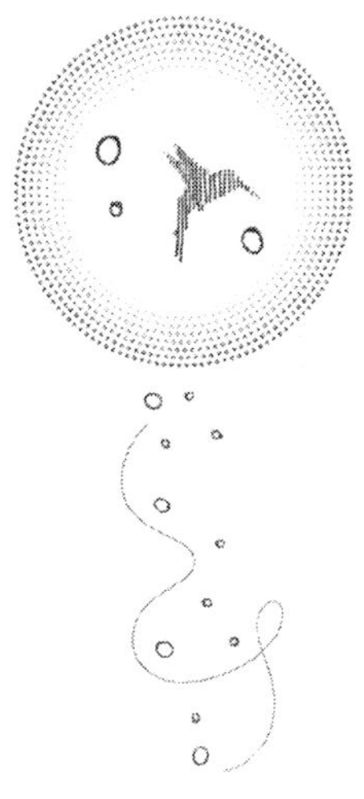

9.

THE MISTERY OF THE WORLDS

"Who better to talk about these matters than Tepatiqui, the guardian between the worlds," Kauyumari began. "He is the one who, day and night, performs incantations and healing chants on trees, dolphins, humans, and goblins alike, upholding the extraordinary possibilities of life on Earth."

"Thank you very much for the kind introduction, Kauyumari. It is a pleasure to be here with all of you on this fine day," Tepatiqui started.

"It fills me with joy to share that many humans are constantly tending their connection to the Wild Spirit, taking on the task of healing the disastrous effects of the domestication of their souls. You may wonder how these humans tackle such a needed feat. Well, let me speak about that, not without first introducing myself properly."

Pili, the tick, was entranced by Tepatiqui's distinctive presence and personality. The curious mushroom evoked a combination of warm feelings and kind-heartedness with a profound strength and intensity—something she had rarely, if ever, witnessed.

Tepatiqui displayed a brownish conical cap with purple and metallic hues. From time to time, the cap reflected shimmering rays of sunlight that made their way through the canopy. The underside of the cap consisted of a series of white and purple gills that converged at the top of the stem. The stem itself, whitish in color and displaying a ring around its midpoint, connected to the moist earth below.

Pili, submerged in the immensity of the details, could not pinpoint what it was that captivated her so much. Tepatiqui radiated a particular aura, something so blatantly obvious that went by unnoticed.

Tepatiqui began.

"I am a member of a select group of organisms that enable a profound and direct connection to the Wild Spirit by way of communion. Through healing and divinatory rituals where my clan is ingested, the human inhabitants of ancient Mexico came to know me as *teonanácatl* or 'flesh of the gods.'

My fungi lineage and I have a long, intimate history with the human species, to the extent that we have played an active role in the evolution of human consciousness. Perhaps this is due to our kinship with the stars that allows us to unveil the uplifting ways of the Wild Spirit in a rather direct, clear manner.

Humans humble enough to come to us and ask for advice are often able to hear the voices of wild nature within themselves. The intimate fungi-human alliance activates a wondrous physiology that brings the clear vision of reality—reality just as it is, amazingly infinite. This is what I refer to as 'the mystery of the worlds.'"

"Taking into consideration this ineffable mystery, the perception of the domesticated human has shrunk to precarious limits," Kauyumari added.

"The incantations of machine sorcerers have programmed fellow citizens to buy into the illusion of separation, while collapsing the many realms into a limited range of material experience," contributed Tuwe, the jaguar warrior.

"With the presence of the Wild Spirit obscured, people miss their chance to experience the beauty and mystery of our beautiful world," continued Tepatiqui. "This point is essential. I could simplify the planetary conundrum we find ourselves in and the fundamental intention of our council by saying that the gargantuan problem we face is largely caused by the way our human kin conceive the world."

"It is here, at the level of perception and worldview, that your admirable work is of tremendous help," commented Kauyumari.

"I'd think so," replied Tepatiqui.

"We know the situation is direly pressing. Even with the havoc caused by domesticated humans, the community of Earth ceaselessly extends its supportive hand. The invitation to return home is always there," the wise deer added, as he looked at Artemio.

Artemio nodded affirmatively. He then closed his eyes and put both hands on his chest in a sign of respect and appreciation.

"I would love to experience your healing, Tepatiqui," expressed Artemio sincerely.

Mushroom and deer looked at each other with an ample smile, in the same way they have been doing from time immemorial when anyone, anywhere, and from their own sovereignty, chooses to release themselves from their shackles.

After a few moments of blessed silence, Tepatiqui continued.

"The human-mushroom communion celebrates our ancestral belonging. Such intimate bond clears a path amongst the complex and often puzzling jungles of the mind. As we traverse these jungles together, the distorted view of the domesticated human in direct contact with all kinds of wild mysteries has no choice but to awaken to the miracle of existence.

In essence, our inter-species communion reveals the exquisite interdependence of creation itself. Then, naked in mind and heart, humans come to terms with the realization that the mystery of the worlds dwells deep within themselves."

A ray of sunshine slipped through the canopy of the surrounding trees. Landing directly on Tepatiqui's cap, the shimmering light produced a rainbow-colored radiance around him. It was as if Sun and jungle agreed with his words.

"Would you say that this realization has to do with a feeling of being part of something so vast and so loving that any attempt to arrive at an explanation is just awkward and inadequate?" asked Artemio.

"Something like that, my dear one," replied Tepatiqui.

The young human shared Pili's fascination with Tepatiqui. Artemio was both utterly curious and noticeably apprehensive in relation to what the healing mushroom referred to as the mystery of the worlds.

"The lush, endless jungles of the Wild Spirit are our origin and destiny," continued Tepatiqui. "And to come to meet oneself so openly, to gaze into our true origin, cuts through the influence of the spell of the machine world and creates an inner reference to continue along the wondrous path of our own lives in beauty and peace.

This is to say that my fungi clan is capable of revealing the sacred within. In the same way that the network of mycelium underneath the soil sustains my being, so a hidden spark of divinity sustains us all.

The direct experience of the sacred awakens the healer dwelling in the depths of the inner jungles. By this I mean that, broadly speaking, accessing the many worlds often brings about profound healing.

The jungle physician procures, with incomparable precision, the experiences needed to unravel the knots of internal conditioning that lead to disease. This, in turn, assists a gradual reconciliation with the levity of life.

Taking the leap into the many worlds, the multiple levels of consciousness where the medicine we are in need of is found, is our birthright. It's vital for the domesticated soul to go beyond ingrained prejudices against my clan and the rest of nature in order to gain access to these medicines.

Let us not be confused. Venturing into the fertile mystery of the Wild Spirit through fungi communion is as natural as water, fire, or wind. After all, the inner healer is but love at a highly refined vibration."

A gust of wind swept the area of the council. The nearby stream flowed easefully, knowing that some humans had been good friends with Tepatiqui and his clan for a long time.

"High-frequency love breaks through all kinds of barriers," Tepatiqui continued.

"As the Wild Spirit's good old friend, the jungle healer weaves connections and networks for the energies of love to roam freely in the hearts and minds of our human kin. Gradually, this process brings an awareness of an immeasurably kind and generous presence that guides and nurtures all beings.

As I mentioned, connecting with the jungle healer and the Wild Spirit allows undoing habitual, machine-like patterns to bring about a more fulfilling life. Naturally, this experience awakens the wild heart of our human sisters and brothers, which in turn engenders a genuine inspiration to stoke the fire of our shared origins.

Communing with my clan, along with many other practices that connect directly to the Wild Spirit, leaves a certain signature or imprint at the level of the heart. This serves as reference and signpost to skillfully navigate the world of everyday life. It is difficult to remain the same person after communing with the flesh of the gods."

"This all sounds wonderful," intervened Narillo, the nine-band armadillo. "I wonder how our human kin has managed to remain faithful to the influence of domestication given the many virtues of your clan and the constant messages of the holy community of nature."

Smiling, Tepatiqui responded.

"It is very important to maintain an intention of respect and humility when facing the many expressions of the Wild Spirit. However effective the healing effects of my fungi family may be, for example, it is necessary that there be a minimum of disposition and openness on the part of our human kin."

"And how is it that the ritual communion with your lineage is not a common practice?" Pili asked a little disconcerted.

"Good question," replied Tepatiqui.

"Domesticated humans often ridicule, and even demonize, everything that defies their own misguided ways. How do you cure someone who's not aware of the disease that corrodes them from the inside?"

"But everything is so simple," said Narillo, as if talking to himself.

"Earth's wild voices are found within the human being since the beginning of time," Tepatiqui continued. "With a clear intention and a safe, caring setting, our inter-species ritual communion amplifies the wild call of reconnection. What is true, good, and beautiful becomes visible once again to the human eye.

In truth, our ritual is but one way to celebrate the mutual belonging of humans, fungi, and the rest of nature. Yet a mightily fascinating one. Coming together in this holy way nurtures body and mind, while allowing the healing presence of the Wild Spirit to manifest."

In a spontaneous outburst of joy, the tropical mockingbird emitted a beautiful, poly-tonal melody that rippled in all directions, caressing the many tendrils of the living jungle. Shortly after, the rhythmic sounds were accompanied by the croaks of a giant toad and the trance-inducing pecking of a woodpecker perched at the top of the cohune palm.

"Life is endlessly recreated in ever-growing spirals," continued Tepatiqui, his voice effortlessly blending with the communal melody. "When coming face to face with the Wild Spirit, the natural response of any being is that of awe, respect, and reverence.

To make the apparent impossibility of the mystery of the worlds a living, breathing reality, it's necessary to cherish the deep yearning for freedom that bubbles forth within all beings. We are all a living expression of something beautifully immeasurable."

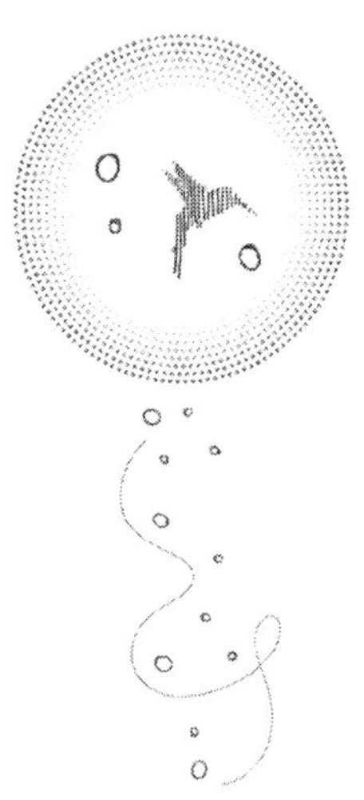

10.

MEDICINE FOR THE BROKEN

The striking shades of orange, red, and pink up in the sky heralded the end of the day. The multi-hued sky swiftly gave way to that window of time where it's difficult to discern whether it is dawn or dusk. This signaled Kauyumari to examine the surroundings once again by sniffing the air in four directions.

In the meantime, Artemio was thoroughly immersed in the ups and downs of his own mind—with that all too familiar mental chatter. Bringing the inner cackling to a halt, an image of the "human fracture" came to him in a flash, accompanied by the conviction that, somehow, it was through those cracks that the mind's chatter made itself present.

Noting the liveliness of his mental dialogue made him realize how it had remained at ease for the entire day. This was not surprising, given the rather unusual events the young man had been involved in.

Again, the image of the human crack made itself present, this time with greater sharpness. Artemio clearly experienced how the fracture spread throughout different parts of his body, particularly affecting his inner left thigh.

"We are not even aware of the sources of our food. We seem to think that it magically appears on the supermarket shelves," Artemio expressed his concern out loud.

It was clear that the issue of food consumption was one of many symptoms of the inner fragmentation felt by Artemio and shared at a collective level. A memory of his old life glued to his office desk, absorbed by the blind compulsion of profit and success, brought an acute mixture of grief and shame.

A pleasant aroma coming from Tonalli, the copal tree, invited him to look up and observe the surroundings. The many beings at the council were looking at him with great compassion.

"It's time," said Tepatiqui, the healer mushroom, in a loving but firm voice.

The council participants intoned in unison a low, muffled sound that Artemio felt like a pleasant tickle all over his body. After some indeterminate amount of time, a cracking sound came, as if something was breaking.

His attention was drawn to Tepatiqui, whose hat appeared to have grown disproportionately to encompass and embrace all council's members. The cap's expansion brought with it a somewhat foul odor, mixed with a smell of wet earth. A ferrous, floury taste invaded Artemio's taste buds.

Soon after, his hands began sweating profusely, while his heart beat in such a way that he could hear it pounding loud and clear.

At that moment, he realized that his senses were significantly sharpened. He became acutely aware of the fading green tones of the jungle. Flying insects were as loud as chirping birds, while the many jungle scents cleared his nostrils and appeared to enlarge his lung capacity. A sensation of discomfort spread throughout his body, just as if he were inhabiting that particular human organism for the first time.

A deep yawn came over him as he focused on the discomfort. Tepatiqui broke the silence with a chant in an unknown language. Moments later, Kauyumari joined.

Like statues made of stone, the council participants stood motionless. Eyes closed. Flashes of white light appeared all around

Artemio. It was then that a fascinating kaleidoscopic vision emerged, following the pace of Tepatiqui's and Kauyumari's chant.

Artemio looked to his right and came face to face with Narillo, the nine-banded armadillo, who was perched right beside him. The armadillo began to merge with Ramón, the breadnut tree, found a few meters (feet) away. The atoms of both creatures seemed to vibrate faster and faster and, like magnets, gave into each other. Their now light bodies melted into one being.

As they merged, the most extraordinary and vibrant colors appeared dancing in the air. The same merging process began to take place all around Artemio. Tuwe, the jaguar, merged with Petra, the opossum; Eshéni, the white-throated magpie, blended with the green iguana and Quispe, the basaltic rock, with the green frog.

Artemio was able to isolate and observe the different events, despite the fact that the mergers and transformations were happening all at once.

Soon, Artemio couldn't distinguish any particular creature. There was no land, air, or anything familiar around him. It wasn't clear to him whether his eyes were open or closed. It didn't matter. The wondrous landscape remained the same—a mass of colors that swirled and danced, forming all sorts of patterns and incredible shapes.

When Artemio thought of joining the spectacle, he swiftly lost all notion of his own body and became part of the multicolored flow. Blue, pink, yellow, red, green, purple, and then all together.

Although as a whole they were part of the same flow, each color and pattern that Artemio was part of maintained its own identity. Everything appeared as a vast and powerful flow, without beginning or end. The young human experienced a taste of freedom.

For a moment, everything and everyone reclaimed its familiar shape. Artemio managed to discern what appeared to be Tuwe spinning in the distance and Kauyumari floating right beside him. The vision again changed from the static world of shapes and boundaries, to the fluid, multi-colored world.

While inhabiting the great kaleidoscopic flow, he discovered that it was possible to transform by way of his own will. He intended to shapeshift into Tuwe, and so he did. While in the vibrant, energetic world, he experienced this as a subtle, yet radical reorganization of his consciousness. In the world of forms, he was able to see and feel like a powerful jaguar. He ran and roared through mountains and jungles, feeling the mighty power of the majestic feline.

He experienced the amazing transformation countless times. Time and again, Artemio was fish, bird, tree, river, cloud, and various mammals. He even became one with the totality of the flow, if just for a precious moment that oddly felt like a very long time. A profound and indescribable sense of belonging, peace, and warmth seized him.

As the vision came, so it vanished. Artemio then appeared sitting facing Tepatiqui at the center of a clearing in the depths of the jungle, illuminated by the flames of a living fire. Tepatiqui vibrated tremendously. It was as if the illustrious mushroom was the host of an infinite number of beings. The energy contained in the vision was almost impossible to bear.

Tepatiqui changed his form, becoming a tall, thin, and resplendent humanoid. The androgynous entity approached Artemio with a friendly smile on their lips, pointing out the cracked areas in his body that, if left unattended, would gravely drain his vital energy.

The young man laid on his back. Standing next to Artemio, the glowing human-like being raised their arms to the sky. As they descended, filaments of light connected the stars with the fragmented areas of Artemio's body. Threads of light also emerged from the Earth to meet Artemio after Tepatiqui touched the ground.

A radiant sphere of celestial and terrestrial energies enveloped the young human. Artemio saw the scene from the outside, as if he was watching a movie.

"The cracks inside you are remnants of innumerable battles through time," began Tepatiqui. "Battles with yourself. Acknowledge them. Respect them for what they are. And bid them farewell. Give yourself permission to do so. You are worthy and of incalculable value, just as you are.

The human being is a wonderful creature with a unique potential, always ready to manifest. The same Sun that shines in the skies and enlivens all life on Earth, is the same Sun that shines within you. Receive the Sun with open arms."

Tepatiqui's face was right next to Artemio's, who felt a mix of deep respect and affection for this being. Tepatiqui's eyes somehow absorbed Artemio's consciousness back into the radiant energy sphere. There, the young human noticed that within the filaments of light that encircled his body traveled even brighter golden seeds that, one by one, were being sown into him.

His attention was caught by one of the cracks. Its blackness swallowed him. An endless avalanche of images of suffering, destruction, and decadence ensued.

Artemio was urged to observe and be fully present with each and every one of the horrific details. Turning his gaze was just beyond his means. Over and over again he witnessed the most atrocious crimes against life. He couldn't bear it any longer. The intensity of the pain was about to break him into a thousand pieces.

A dark mist invaded him, bringing with it his greatest fear; to be lost in suffering forever. The mist came out of his mouth and took the form of an individual very similar to himself but vaporous and dark. Artemio understood that this ghost-like character represented the sum total of the cracks inside him. His greatest fear personified was one with the suffering of the whole world.

About to lose any trace of conscious awareness, Artemio heard Tepatiqui's voice in the distance: "Although the sky might be cloudy, the Sun always shines with its light."

Tepatiqui's words echoed through the dark night, leaving a trace of a cleansing fragrance in their wake. This allowed Artemio to regain a bit of composure, realizing that he was laying on the ground, in a fetal position. His hand, moving by itself, purposefully touched the Earth.

The Earth provided him a sense of stability, of groundedness, even of deep care and nourishment. "The Earth Mother," he thought to himself. In spite of all the madness, the Earth had never left.

Tepatiqui's words were still echoing in Artemio's mind. "Even if I'm unable to see the light, the Sun is also here…Father Sun," this time whispering to himself.

The energies of Earth and Sun provided safe refuge. Taking a couple of deep breaths, the young man stood up and faced the menacing figure. Without further ado, Artemio mustered the courage to speak.

"I've traversed the valley of my worst fears. I have felt the ghastly effects of the spell of the machine world and the great suffering that comes with it. And yet I know now that I have nothing to fear. There's nothing to be lost. What is truly valuable can never be taken away. What is that you want? What do you need from me? I see you."

As Artemio connected more and more with the breath, the fearsome figure began to take a more familiar shape, until it transformed into Artemio's twin. Finally, with a gentle smile on its face, the once turmoiled ghost completely vanished.

It was now possible for Artemio to fully take rest in the refuge of Father Sun and Mother Earth. There, exhausted, the vision of the energy sphere enveloping his body returned. Tepatiqui was by his side.

The humanoid mushroom smiled, whispering in Artemio's ear something he couldn't quite grasp. Tepatiqui burst into a powerful laughter that made the whole scene disappear.

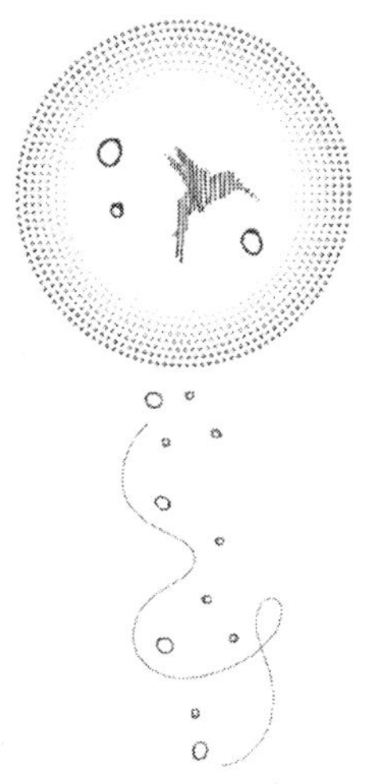

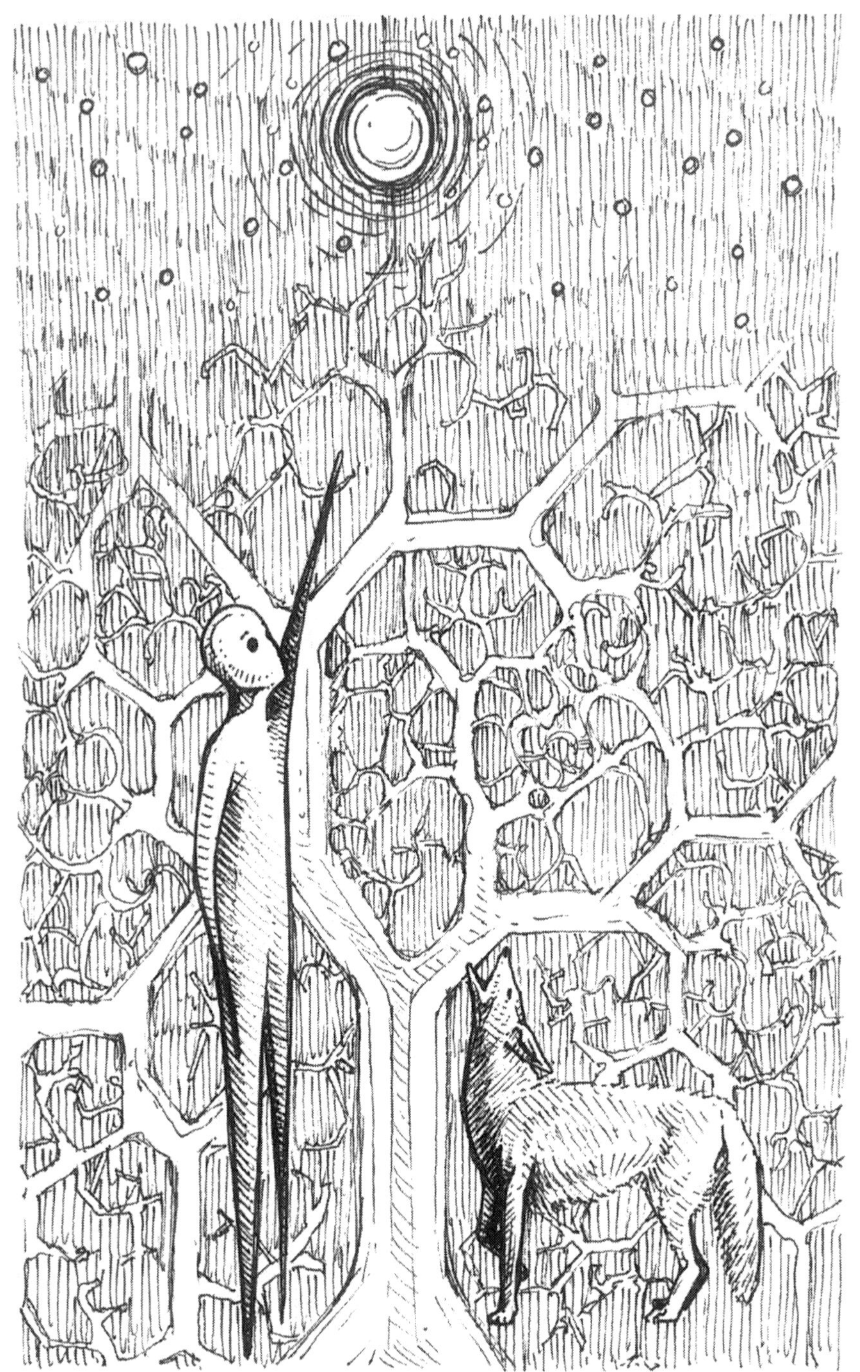

11.
COSMIC TRIBE

The fresh morning sunlight bathed the council participants. The green of the jungle had regained its vibrancy. The dawn chorus from the region's rich variety of birds was in full swing.

The melodic sounds gradually restored the energy of the group after the portentous night-time journeys, dissipating the last remnants of sluggishness. Artemio was particularly cheerful due to the onset of a new day.

Kauyumari invited the group to find their inner refuge and spend a few moments in silence together. The wise deer encouraged them to actively replenish the refined state of connection cultivated during the council, knowing that a calm mind serves as a well-tuned instrument through which the Earth resonates Her healing presence.

The sounds of the jungle became even more audible, the same sounds that provided the gathering with high doses of clarity and wellbeing. It is known that wild sounds such as the flow of a stream or the chirping of crickets or a bird's song maintain an optimal state of health and promote happiness.

After a while, the different creatures went from silence in repose to conscious movement. They stretched and moved their bodies in unison, following certain soft and undulating patterns that reduced muscular tension and stimulated circulation. Artemio surprised himself by following the group's movements without much effort. The energy levels were palpably lighter and clearer.

"I believe that the more humans consciously relate with us and with the rest of wild nature, the greater the likelihood of them catching a glimpse of their own essence," interceded Ramón, the breadnut tree.

"I very much agree," answered Kauyumari. "Can you think of a strategy to help counteract the growing aversion that our human kin have towards nature?"

Ramón reflected for a few moments before answering.

"Trees play an important role, since we are one of the few beings that aren't overlooked by the domesticated eye of our human kin. For this reason, we can more readily teach them about an essential disposition that serves as cure for the unfounded fear and aversion toward nature, stillness.

My tree kin have refined the art of peaceful abiding. We stand firm yet flexible despite the madness that often surrounds us. We endeavor to nurture life in the midst of the darkest night or under the brilliance of Father Sun."

"And how is it that you have refined this admirable capacity?" asked Kaninde, the green macaw.

"The secret lays in deeply honoring our roots so that we can stretch our branches toward the heavens. This makes our tree people a resilient and welcoming abode where joy and life thrive," declared Tonalli, the copal tree.

"We invite our human brothers and sisters to caress the Earth with bare feet while keeping their gaze high up to the Sun. Their feet in direct contact with the Earth reminds them of their origins, their gaze up to the sky invites the necessary discernment to choose life at every step."

"Maintaining a peaceful, equanimous stance is fundamental for our ability to manifest life and be the gracious hosts of light and joy that we are," continued Ramón.

"Just as inner stillness acts as a bridge between humans and the rest of nature, conscious movement also reconnects," added Dellwi, the earthworm.

"Please, tell us more, Dellwi," commented Kauyumari.

"The presence or absence of flexibility is related to the posture from which the world is perceived. In fact, compulsive behaviors that often bring violence and abuse to our communities are associated with knots or obstructions at the physical level."

Dellwi's remark reminded the young Artemio of his fascination with cement—rigid, square, and grey, just like the machine-like compulsions that ruled over his daily life.

Ruminating on his old life, Artemio felt sincere compassion for the past version of himself that did the best he could. Perhaps, for the first time, he was capable of looking at himself without much judgment, for he could envision just how limited his take on life had been.

"In addition to relieving stress and helping to regulate emotions, the practice of conscious movement enlivens the bodies and minds of our human kin," continued Dellwi.

"The wild, self-healing intelligence of mountains and rivers also oversees blood circulation, digestion, and breathing in the human ecosystem. Through conscious movement, this same intelligence brings fluidity and harmony to the body and mind, in turn promoting more ethical and empathetic attitudes."

Artemio glimpsed an agile figure crossing quickly on all fours from one side of the circle to the other, to sit next to Kauyumari.

Chirich, the coyote, was known for her musical gifts and enigmatic and furtive behavior. Her pointy muzzle and sharp teeth, along with her slender body and cosmopolitan aura contributed to her reputation.

The truth was that Chirich enjoyed an intimate and playful relationship with the Wild Spirit. It was well known that Chirich and Tepatiqui, the healer mushroom, spent days together, sharing stories about their fantastic adventures in the many worlds.

Once comfortably settled in place, the furtive coyote asked Artemio about the previous night with a mischievous smile. Tepatiqui grinned.

Artemio, somewhat apprehensive, took a deep breath. He felt as if an invisible veil covered him from head to toe, and that his words would tear his comfortable cover, leaving him completely vulnerable. Despite the coyotes' often dubious reputation, he felt that Chirich was trustworthy.

"Mm, it was OK," replied the young man timidly.

The comment was followed by a wave of laughter from the participants of the council. After clearing his throat a couple of times, Artemio tried again.

"First of all, I would like to thank you all for the opportunity to be here and learn from you, be healed by you. I would especially like to thank Kauyumari for his kindness and support and Tepatiqui for opening my eyes to the miracle of existence. To each and every one of you ... thank you from the bottom of my heart."

Artemio's voice vacillated due to the cascade of feelings piling up in his chest. Nonetheless, he persevered.

"Anything I could tell you would not do justice to my experience last night. I feel extremely fortunate to have been able to experience firsthand the mystery of the worlds. It was something I will never forget. Even if I wanted to, my life could not be the same as before.

Perhaps, for the first time, I recognize some greatness in me, and at the same time know how small I am before the vastness of the mystery. Will it be possible for this greatness to take root in my life? How can I go about doing that?"

"You partake in the essence of the planet, the galaxy, and the whole universe. Your existence is created and recreated at every moment through every tiny event that takes place in the eternal present," Chirich replied. Her every word filled with kindness and care.

"The crickets in the fields, the birds that cruise the skies, the majesty of the mountains, the tireless winds, the stars that bathe us with their light, the magical songs of the whales. We are all part of the same team. And each and every one of us is a miniature expression of the whole team. We are a cosmic tribe.

If you take this into consideration, it is difficult to distinguish where you begin and where you end. The loving, tangled vastness of the Wild Spirit is your true home."

Artemio remembered vividly the events of the previous night in which he had merged with other beings and was one with the multicolored flow. This intimate interconnection had been registered in the depths of his heart.

"Outwardly different, inwardly the same," Artemio said to himself internally, smiling, as he listened to Chirich's comments.

"In the eternity of the present moment, the dance between giving and taking is perpetually celebrated, the same dance that guides the adventure of consciousness on this planet," continued the coyote. As we become familiar with the secret of inter-being, with all the joyful trials that it entails, we begin to awaken to who we really are."

Artemio understood at a cellular level that the visions in which he transformed into different beings had not only been inspiring and life-affirming, but each transformation carried within it a precious medicine. This wild medicine had been readily available since his arrival at the council.

"I guess each and all creatures represent aspects of my own self. And I'm part of them," Artemio said aloud, still digesting the far-reaching consequences of the conversation.

Chirich, Kauyumari, and Tepatiqui looked at each other in a sign of satisfaction.

The cracks that Artemio noticed in his fellow city dwellers were largely the result of estranged tracts of wild nature, of forgotten people, human and non-human alike.

He now had a better grasp of the brokenness he had felt most of his life. He had ceaselessly sought for an answer in all the wrong places.

He now began to grasp that the variety of beings that make up the community of life on Earth made up his truer Self, all of them frequencies that carried gifts and potentialities capable of restoring the totality of his humanity.

Artemio reflected on the wisdom and leadership of the deer; the patience and strength of the rock; the agility and authority of the jaguar; the conscious listening and broad perspective of birds; the sacredness and spiritual healing of mushrooms; the patience and stillness of trees, and much more. All qualities and virtues of a more fulfilled and whole human.

"Of course, humans are wild members of the community of Earthly creatures. Don't ever forget that," said Chirich to Artemio. "All of us are accountable for the totality of the planetary family. We depend on each other in the most amazing ways you can imagine."

Silence reigned for a long time, out of which arose an exquisite sense of fellowship and camaraderie amongst the attendees. They laughed, shared stories, and had a good time.

Artemio looked around with the curiosity and joy of a newborn, as if experiencing the world for the first time. With such lightness in mind and heart, it was clear to him that direct contact with wild nature engendered the healing frequencies that restored his long-sought fullness.

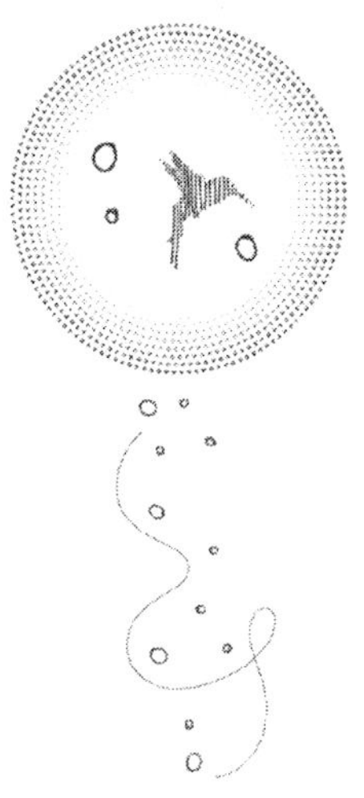

12.

INFINITE WILD GLOW

Kauyumari announced that the Council of All Beings was coming to an end.

"Dear friends, I thank each of you once again for your invaluable participation and inspiring presence. It has been an eventful and fruitful journey. We've shared our voices and opened our hearts, our dreams and yearnings, and we've laughed and cried together. The omens have signaled the way. We even have brother Artemio here with us."

Kauyumari proceeded to personally thank the various speakers for their valued contributions and for nurturing, with their words, deeds, and intentions, the Wild Spirit, the source of existence.

"The history of our community, the many peoples that inhabit this jungle, the destruction of our homes, the vicious confusion of our human kin, the soul's domestication, and the good fortune to be alive in this beautifully uncertain period of transition and change of our planetary home—all this has been part of our council.

We know that the medicine to the human insanity that erodes our communities is found by way of reclaiming their wild place in the natural order. The realization of their true ecological niche sets forth a brighter future for us all."

With this last comment, the elder deer referred to the confusion and difficulty of the domesticated human to see itself as part of the living web of peoples, both human and non-human, that populate the Earth. Haunted by the spell of the machine world, the so-called modern humans suffer from a chronic amnesia of the sacred, from an oblivion of the ancestral memory that respects, honors, and cares for the community of life.

On the other hand, the medicine that strips away confusion and brings clear vision was faithfully represented by the council participants themselves; a respectful, direct engagement with the many expressions of wild nature.

It's as if every wild creature safeguarded a small flask full of their own essence, of their remedy, in their own hearts. And that remedy is transmitted from an open heart to an open heart.

In spite of its effective simplicity and widespread distribution, the medicine capable of transforming the most obnoxious refuse into the fertile soil of a flourishing life, seems to go entirely overlooked by those under the spell of the machine world.

All the while, with patience and care, the Earth Mother has refined Her medicines for eons, currently expressing an unparalleled degree of efficacy and potency. With each lunar cycle, the antidote becomes ever more effective.

A single drop of the elixir of the Wild Spirit would be enough to release the entire human family from the spell. But for that precious drop to enter the human heart, it needs to be summoned from the depths. Once active, the elixir would irreversibly manifest the beauty and creativity of the Earth in each and every one of Her children.

"Friends, let us take a moment to honor the urgent request of the forest keepers to end the suffering of all beings," continued Kauyumari. "It is because of their fervor and devotion to life that opportunities for dialogue and reconciliation such as our council are made possible."

"This council is our offering to the Wild Spirit," expressed Tuwe, the jaguar warrior, after some moments of silence. "It is our communal way to strengthen the plea of the forest keepers.

One of the formulas to invoke and activate the healing presence of wild nature is simply to nourish it, to nurture and celebrate that which sustains us all."

"The Wild Spirit is not a cosmic errand boy, but responds to the intention imprinted in our actions," intervened Kauyumari. "An intention free from imposition that takes into consideration the welfare of others is high grade food for the Wild Spirit. Curiously, when this food is offered selflessly, we receive a gift of deep fulfilment and contentment. These growing cycles of generosity make of life an endless poem."

"We offer all the experiences of this council at the feet of the Wild Altar," intervened Quispe, the ancient basaltic rock.

As if moved by an invisible hand, those present reconvened the ritual circle. Closing their eyes, they faced the center of the circle. Moments later, the energy of the group was concentrated in such a way that the jungle itself responded.

An avalanche of wild sounds from all directions was heard, coalescing in the sudden appearance of a multicolored bundle at the center of the circle. From the bundle arose a column of rotating air that stretched towards the sky, shimmering with a rainbow-colored glow.

Quispe emitted a vibration that made the Earth shake from within, a movement that the participants accompanied with an audible and long exhalation. Together, vibration and sound lured the whirlwind to be swallowed back to the Earth.

The multicolored bundle at the circle's center shone even brighter. Like a seed about to sprout, the bundle contained the energetic signature of the whole jungle. Moments later, the iridescent energy at the center of the circle was also absorbed by the Earth, at the precise moment that all sound and vibration ceased.

"Thank you very much, Quispe," said Kauyumari.

"With pleasure," Quispe replied.

With this offering, the Council of All Beings had come to an end.

And so, the attendees began to part ways, but not before bidding farewell to each other. The green iguana headed for her rocky house on the other side of the hills, the same direction that the macaw of the same color was heading. The army of acacia ants formed a single line and headed back to their tree house. Petra, the opossum, and the nine-banded armadillo parted together in search of something to eat. In this way, the rest of the many beings returned to their families.

Tonalli, the copal tree, Quispe, the basaltic rock, and Ramón, the breadnut tree, simply diverted their attention to their daily tasks. Eshéni, the white-throated magpie, Tuwe, the jaguar warrior, and Tepatiqui, the healer mushroom, affectionally bid Artemio farewell and expressed their care and trust in him. Kauyumari seemed to be talking to someone in the distance.

In the midst of it all, Artemio remained in his place, surrounded by fading squawks, buzzes, caws, growls, squeaks, croaks, chirps, and more. A particular hiss or soft whistle caught his attention.

The eerie sound became louder and louder, as Artemio felt a tingling all over his body, but especially at the crown of his head. He looked up and observed trillions of tiny bubbles floating toward him from beyond the treetops, as if a rain of tiny stars were falling on his head. The little stars made his head part open, or somehow grow and expand.

Artemio found himself inhabiting the vibrant multicolored world he became acquainted with the previous night. This time he was attracted by a particular field of colors whose vibrational signature made for an irresistible invitation.

While there, he felt an incredibly placid and loving warmth. This heat emanated a soothing, peaceful glow that seemed to extend into infinity, creating an exquisite series of dancing forms and patterns. There was nothing but dancing golden light everywhere.

At the climax of Artemio's bliss state, the golden landscape gave way to two distinct images. The first one showed Artemio in his routine life from work to home and back, surrounded by people so immersed in the spell of the machine world that they fiercely defended their comfortable prison-like way of life. In the second image, Artemio saw himself accompanied by Nool, the elder who, in a dream, taught him about the evolving creativity of the Earth.

Both images gradually faded. A detailed recapitulation of the series of transformative events he had undergone since that memorable dream ensued. Each image and experience were presented from different angles, with the intention of being thoroughly assimilated by Artemio.

The recapitulation was a long, demanding process. Then, the images just lost their appeal. Artemio gradually opened his eyes. In doing so, he found himself back in the jungle in the company of Kauyumari.

"Ah, I see that our friend Nool is still doing his thing," said the elder deer with a smile.

"How do you know each other?" Artemio asked calmly, admitting that everything was possible in the jungles of the Wild Spirit.

Kauyumari remained silent for a few moments. Then he began to speak with a gentle, comforting voice.

"This life is a precious gift. This gift allows for the precious opportunity to choose. Every moment, every circumstance, serves as a portal that leads to the uncertain yet amazing paths of the Wild Spirit or along the beaten track where fear and reactivity abound.

The simplicity and levity of a wild person has little to do with returning or clinging to a cruelty-free past where everything was perfect, but has everything to do with the choice to free oneself from the heaviness of the heart.

Audacity is a wild person's best friend. Time and again, the wild one errs on the side of the liberation and flourishing of all life, even though all odds may appear against this. This is the reason why seeing with the eyes of the wild heart is vital. The wise and loving heart serves as a faithful guide that cuts through the illusion of the machine world to come into contact with the mystery of things as they are."

Artemio listened attentively to Kauyumari, longing for a steady connection with the Wild Spirit, for a gradual and thorough rewilding of the heart.

"The clear vision that springs forth from a wild heart provides the spaciousness to act in a freer way, unrestrained from rigidity and prejudice," the wise deer continued. "This spacious place within, an inner prairie if you will, allows for respect and reverence to surface and nurture all our relations.

Above all, the wild call of nature summons the practice of gentleness, generosity, and kindness that is our birthright. By this I mean that nature tirelessly reminds us that love is always an option. Love awaits us with open arms in the wild depths of the heart and in the wild landscapes of this precious Earth."

Bringing his face closer to the young human, as someone who wants to entrust a precious secret, Kauyumari continued.

"Artemio, in you as in your entire human family there's a precious capacity to choose. A wild and liberated life is readily available at every single turn."

A muffled, buzzing sound caught Artemio's attention. Once again, he felt the top of his head part open, out of which a radiant, white hummingbird emerged. The buzzing sound of the bird's wings left a multicolored wake as it flew around visiting nearby flowers.

After a few twists and turns, the prodigious hummingbird stopped right in front of Artemio. The swift flutter echoed throughout his body, but was particularly resonant at the level of his heart. Moments later, the little bird came even closer, as if its small beak sought to pollinate the heart of the young human.

A warm sensation of tender joy returned, this time bringing with it the two images of Artemio's old life and its recent transformation. A transcendental decision lay ahead: to return to the comfort of the known or to delve deeper into the wild glow.

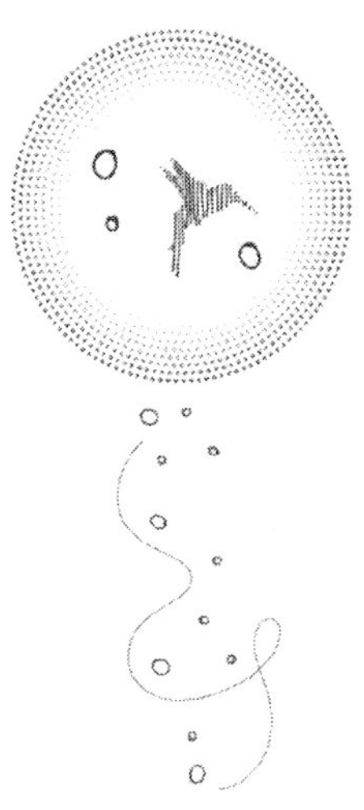